CONJURING THE WITCH

JESSICA LEONARD

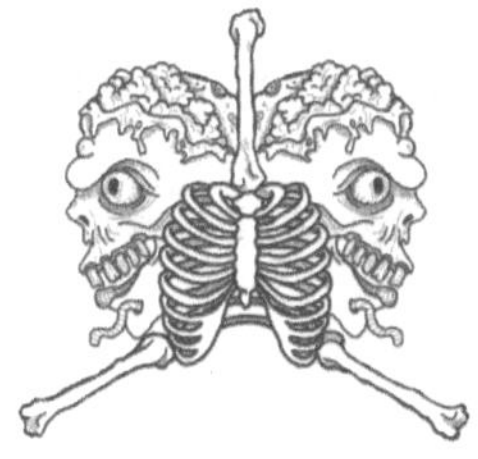

Ghoulish Books
an imprint of Perpetual Motion Machine Publishing
San Antonio, Texas

Conjuring the Witch

ISBN: 978-1-943720-84-2

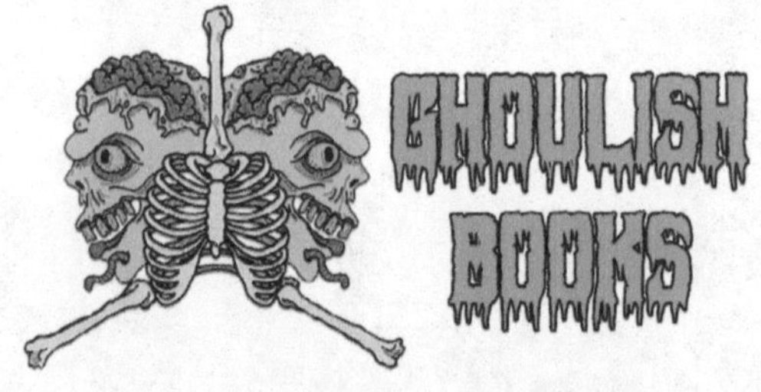

www.GhoulishBooks.com

Cover by Matthew Revert

ALSO BY THE AUTHOR

Antioch

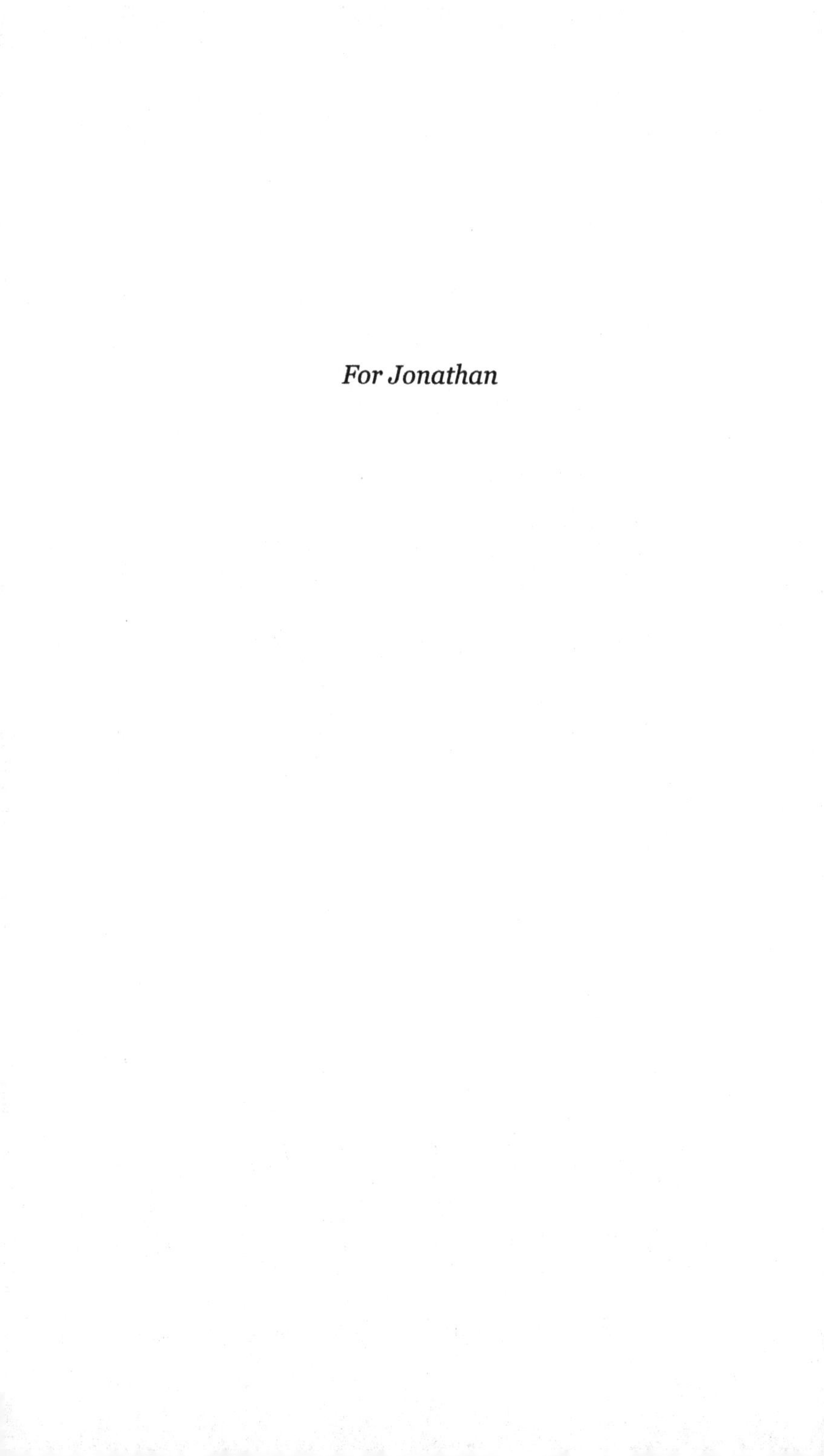

For Jonathan

CHAPTER 1

"THERE ARE WITCHES in the woods."

The reverend told them this every Sunday, and while some assumed he was being figurative, there were others among the congregation who weren't so sure. They cast long looks out into the thick green brush that surrounded the eastern and southern sides of the Lilin Assembly of Our Lord and wondered, *Are they out there*?

There was a great glowing cross on the outside of the church—right in the center of the east side—that faced into the forest. Its bright pale-blue light illuminated the trees and created new and complex shadows where nature never intended them to be. This was their defense against the witches. And even those who didn't really believe there was anyone—let alone a witch—out there, felt a sense of comfort knowing the bold LED force field protected them.

Steve and Nicole Warby had joined the church a year ago, not long after moving to Lilin. Steve's father, Russ, had moved his family away when Steve was only three to grow his law practice. Russ had always assumed Steve would follow in his footsteps and one day he would call his office Warby and Warby. Warby and Warby was Russ' greatest dream, and though Steve would never say it out loud, he harbored irrational guilt that moving back to Lilin to become a farmer had killed his father. That his heart stopped from pure grief instead of cholesterol and stress. Steve also believed he'd had no choice but to move. His grandfather had farmed this land, and something was always tugging at him to return. The earth itself was calling him to turn it over and find what was beneath. Earth was funny that way. And when Steve stumbled across the tiny church by the woods, everything simply felt right. He didn't know if his grandfather had attended the church, or even if the building had been built while he was alive, but still. It felt right.

Nicole started out in the decaying farmhouse they moved to with good intentions. She planted a small vegetable garden in the side yard, but halfway through the season she let it go to weeds. The weather was hot, stifling and thick with humidity which regularly drove the heat index to record highs. Steve understood, though he himself worked outside every day. It was in his blood. This is what he'd been Called to do. Nicole didn't know her Calling yet. Her blood held nothing more than plasma, cells, and platelets. There was no ancestral dirt drifting through her veins. The Lilin Assembly of Our Lord filled most of her days—between the women's group and their meetings and various volunteering and fundraising—even so, she did those things only because they were there to be done, not because she was called to do them.

She'd been happy enough to move to Lilin. There was nothing anchoring her to any location in particular. Nicole's own father had been a truck driver—or so her mother told her. He was a traveler. She thought about her dad from time to time, tried to picture who he must be. To her, he was the deafening abrupt blare of a truck horn and soft yellow headlights drifting down the highway at night. He was a ghost.

Communication between Nicole and her mother dwindled once she moved out at 18, not that there had been much to begin with. Sharon Lyons was not the sort of mother who baked, or sewed costumes for the school pageant, or stayed up late talking to her daughter about boys. She was the sort of mother who went to bars, bought TV dinners, and was an advocate for giving her daughter "privacy." Nicole did not think about her mother from time to time—or at all, really. And that was okay. She had considered telling folks in her new home that she was an orphan, but she knew Steve would contradict her.

The Lilin Assembly of Our Lord women's group met every Tuesday evening at 7pm, late enough to still have a family dinner beforehand. The number of women in the group fluctuated at times, however usually there were only four. They were small, and they seemed to like it small.

"Any new business?" Sara Douglas asked. Sara was the group leader. Her husband, Paul, was the head of the church's Council, and if that made Sara the *de facto* women's group leader no one knew, even so, it certainly didn't hurt.

"I'd like to hold a bake sale," Donna Martin answered. "We need new choir robes."

"Okay, I second that," said Charity Cole, because she was also in the choir and the number one rule of church organizations is to protect your own.

Nicole Warby was not listening. Instead, she was watching a silverfish scuttle across the slate-blue carpet of Sara's living room and wondering why they held meetings there instead of at the church, which was more centrally located to most everyone. No other group used the church on Tuesdays. By design, all the various groups and committees met on different nights in order to keep at least one parent at home with the children. It encouraged church members to be more active by taking away excuses. It also encouraged, Nicole felt, members to have children. She was the only member of the women's group without any children, something she felt keenly each time someone asked her or her husband when they were going to start a family. Nicole would always say something vague about timing, or finances. The truth was, she wasn't sure she wanted children at all. She didn't know how to parent, and a part of her would always wonder if she, like her father before her, was a traveler—unable to stay and nurture. If

Steve had impressed anything upon her during their time together, it was that blood was thick, unchanging, and undeniable.

"If there's nothing else, let's move on to the Bible study," Sara said. "Nicole, I believe you have tonight's scripture."

Nicole smiled and picked up her Bible from the coffee table. She knew the only reason Sara would mention her would be for the weekly scripture.

"Tonight's good word comes from the book of Judges, chapter four. This is the story of Deborah, one of the Judges of Israel." Nicole cleared her throat and launched into her reading. "Now Deborah, a prophet, the wife of Lappidoth, was leading Israel at that time. She held court under the Palm of Deborah between Ramah and Bethel in the hill country of Ephraim, and the Israelites went up to her to have their disputes decided."

"I hate all the Old Testament names. I never know who they're talking about," Charity complained.

"Shush," Sara warned. She chose the scriptures based on a book she'd purchased about women from the Bible, which came highly recommended by a Christian Mommy blog she followed more religiously than the religion she practiced.

"Is that normal? For a woman to be leading?" Donna asked.

"Certainly not," Sara snapped. Unscripted conversation felt like chaos and chaos felt like a strong hand closing inside her chest.

"Deborah was the only female judge in the Bible," Charity said, smiling brightly, pleased to have something to contribute.

"You're right," Nicole said, and read on. "Deborah sent for Barak, son of Abinoam from Kedesh in Naphtali, and said to him, 'The Lord, the God of Israel, commands you: "Go, take with you ten thousand men of Naphtali and Zebulun and lead them up to Mount Tabor. I will lead

Sisera, the commander of Jabin's army, with his chariots and his troops to the Kishon River and give him into your hands."' Barak said to her, 'If you go with me, I will go; but if you don't go with me, I won't go.' 'Certainly I will go with you,' said Deborah. 'But because of the course you are taking, the honor will not be yours, for the Lord will deliver Sisera into the hands of a woman.' So Deborah went with Barak to Kedesh." Nicole closed her Bible and leaned back against the couch, satisfied with herself for pronouncing all the strange names without stumbling. And if she'd said some of them wrong, no one was going to contradict her.

"I don't get it," Charity said.

The room stayed silent. Nicole's smile turned to stone as she waited for someone to speak. She didn't want to be the one to start the discussion. Some archaic rule of order made her believe it was bad form for the one who read the verse to also be the one to begin the discussion. And besides, she knew Sara was waiting for the appropriate moment to pounce.

"It's perfectly simple, Charity," Sara began, taking a slow sip of water. "Deborah is only leading because a man has failed. If a man was able to step up into the role he was born to fill, Deborah wouldn't be leading anyone."

"Deborah was a prophet," Donna reminded. "God doesn't make someone a prophet as a Plan B."

"And she was a judge," Charity said. "What's the point?"

"I think the point is that when someone hesitates, when they lose the faith or their faith falters, they aren't going to be rewarded." This was from Donna. She looked to Sara for approval, but Sara was looking at Nicole.

Sara cleared her throat and took another sip of water. "Do you think that's right, Nicole?"

Nicole didn't know what to say, she didn't know why Sara was singling her out. "I think it's worth discussing. After all, if we didn't know anyone's gender in the story, or if it was strictly about two men, I think that's what we'd take from it. That assurance is rewarded, and hesitance is punished."

"They aren't both men," Sara stated.

"No, but how much do we think gender plays a role in it?" Charity asked.

"I'd say quite a bit," said Sara. "God created men and women separately and for different purposes. If we were interchangeable, then why bother making us different at all?"

"That's true," said Charity. "So, what is the purpose of having a female prophet?"

"Perhaps it's God's way of telling women they're worthy of being such. That we aren't lesser," Donna suggested.

"That," Sara said, "is a good point. Of course, we aren't lesser, we are distinctly different." Sara allowed her gaze to fall away from Nicole and back to the room at large. "Deborah shows us that women can be devout and brave."

Nicole was satisfied enough with this conclusion. She'd been thinking for weeks about how she might take a larger role in the church, something not directly associated with the women's group. She believed there must be more for her, more that God wanted from her. Every day her husband left for the fields and every evening he returned, and he was content. On Sundays he would rest. They would go to church and then Nicole would make a big Sunday Meal—some sort of roasted meat with vegetables—and he would sigh because his contentment was so enormous he had to let some of it out or else he might explode. And Nicole was fine. She was not unhappy, but neither was she content. The rest of the women would chat about their sewing projects and their children's extracurriculars and the volunteering they did at the food bank that week . . . and they, too, seemed fulfilled.

After she left Sara's house that night, Nicole drove to the church and sat in the parking lot, her attention focused on that Holy blue light. If she stared into it long enough, the world around her would shimmer and blur at the edges, become less real. Sometimes she would see shapes moving in the darkness around her, probably animals scurrying off to their dens for the night. Tonight, she thought about Deborah. The world recessed and the blue light convexed toward her, swallowed her.

The silence of the evening hummed. There was no breeze, and all the leaves were more still-life than actual life. Nicole stopped breathing because the sound of the air whispering through her respiratory system was sacrilegious.

The smallest *tappity-tap* skittered across the hood of her car. The sound snapped her back into reality, and she blinked a few times to clear the residual blue-red from her vision. Another clatter, and this time Nicole saw a pebble skip across the hood. She looked around the dark parking lot but didn't see anyone. Grabbing her keys from the ignition, she stepped out into the night and hugged herself as defense against the newly brisk air.

"Hello?" Nothing but silence answered her.

"Probably a squirrel," she muttered, and the sound of her own voice calmed her. She stepped toward the woods. Not so much to search for the source of the rocks as to get a better look at the cross. As Nicole neared the forest, she heard a rustling out amongst the trees. The wind returned and whistled past her ears; she squinted to see what might be out there, and for a second, she thought she heard her name carried on the breeze. The back of her neck prickled as the phantom voice of the reverend echoed in her mind. *There are witches in the woods.*

"No thanks," Nicole whispered, and jogged back to her car. For the first time she wondered how far the woods went, how many miles of unbroken wilderness existed right here at the edge of the most human of all buildings—the church.

CHAPTER 2

IN THE WARBY kitchen there was a round wooden dining table with four matching wooden chairs surrounding it. Steve sat at the one which faced the window; he stared out into the dark backyard and thought about nothing. On Tuesday nights he'd gotten into the habit of sitting and staring. It felt nice. And he couldn't be so idle when Nicole was home. She'd worry. She'd ask what was wrong and try to make conversation with him. Nothing was wrong, at least not anything that Steve could pinpoint. He just liked the feeling of being inanimate every now and again.

When it was almost time for Nicole to be getting home, he began coming back to himself. It would happen first in his mind. Some little thought would invade. Today it was about the fields. It was September and the corn harvest had begun later than usual. The world was changing. The seasons were not moving the way they once did when his grandfather had managed the land. Rainy and dry seasons were not as reliable. Things were shifting. It was probably cause for concern on a more global scale, yet Steve mostly found it frustrating. His mind didn't run on a global scale. He just wanted the weather to cooperate.

He heard Nicole's car crunching up the gravel driveway and he cleared his throat. Steve blinked a few times, walked to the refrigerator, and pulled out a Budweiser. Something to do, to make it look like he'd been doing anything other than dissociating for hours.

“I’m home,” Nicole called as she walked through the back door.

“Me too,” Steve said. “How was it tonight?”

“Same as ever.” Nicole sat at the table and smiled at her husband. “Did you call your mom tonight?”

“Ah, no.” Steve looked into the mouth of his can.

“She called me a couple days ago, but she wants to talk to you. She only calls me because she knows I’ll answer.”

“You don’t have to answer.”

Nicole glared until Steve relented and met her eyes. “I know, I know. I’ll call her tomorrow. It’s too late now.”

“She just misses you.”

“She has plenty.”

“That isn’t the point.”

He knew it wasn’t. He didn’t need to say it.

“She thinks I keep you from calling, that I’m keeping you away, and that’s not fair to me.”

He took a long pull from his drink and Nicole got herself a single-serve plastic bottle of cranberry juice. “Hey, Steve?”

“Yeah?”

“I was thinking, do you suppose maybe I could join the church council?”

Steve laughed.

“Seriously,” Nicole said, trying to hide the wound his laughter inflicted.

“Oh, sorry. But, no. I don’t think you could. The council is senior members of the church. Not to mention there aren’t any women on it. Pretty sure that’s a rule.”

Nicole’s mouth became a tight little bud as she tried to stay calm. She hadn’t known how much she wanted to be on the council until she’d said it out loud. Tears stung the corners of her eyes. “We were just reading about Deborah tonight, and she was a leader. And a judge and a prophet too.” Her voice shook a little and Steve was suddenly afraid this was going to become a long conversation. He loved his wife and tried to avoid conflict at all costs. Conversation was often conflict in disguise.

"I'm sure that's all true," Steve said. "But, unless I'm mistaken, you're not a prophet. And, honey, I'm not even on the council. Everyone on it has been at this church forever, their fathers were on the council before them. It's a seniority thing. Nothing personal."

"You could ask, though. At the men's meeting tomorrow night. You could ask Paul about it. It might be that they'd like a woman on the council, and they've just never had one volunteer." Nicole smiled; certain she was correct.

"Wouldn't it show more initiative if you talked to Paul about it yourself?"

"You'll already be with him. Please, Steve? I think this will be really good for me. I just know I'm being called to do this. I know it."

Steve stayed silent. He tried his hardest to fit in with the other men at the church and a big part of that was not calling any attention to himself. He was seen as steady, reliable, and, most of all, not bothersome. Unexpectedly insisting that his wife be a senior member of the church was going to be bothersome, he knew it. He quickly weighed the pros and cons of the situation. He concluded that not doing this would make his wife unhappy, and when she was unhappy things could get difficult around the house. Clothes might go unwashed, dishes uncleaned, dinner uncooked.

"Okay," he conceded. "I'll bring it up to Paul. But listen, I'm not going to push. If he says no, then that's the end of it. You hear me?"

"Absolutely!" Nicole clapped her hands and hopped up and down like a child presented with a treat. "I just know they're going to say yes. Remember to bring up Deborah. That's important."

"You got it. Deborah the prophet."

"And leader. And judge."

That night Nicole took a long hot bath and felt something she assumed was contentment as she got into bed next to her husband. This could be a fresh start for her. She felt reborn by the possibility of new opportunities. Maybe next year she'd try gardening again. She leaned over and kissed Steve goodnight before snuggling down into the covers. She pulled them up to her ears and let the heat from her bath-warmed body radiate out to the bed, and in turn the cool sheets shared their chill with her.

Steve stayed awake for several hours, unable to shake the thought that this was a terrible idea. It'd end up just like the vegetable garden, a strong start and a miserable finish. And he'd be to blame for it, on both sides. Nicole would be unhappy he brought her here and the church would be unhappy that he'd insisted his flake of a wife be on the most important group in the church. He tossed in bed; it was too hot.

He knew many of the men in the church had a very traditional view of family in general and of women in particular. Women were there to cook and clean and have babies. And men were there to lead. He didn't know if he entirely agreed or disagreed. He didn't want to think about it if he didn't have to. He loved the church as if it was an entity all its own, alive and breathing. When he thought of that smallish wooden building with its fierce and blazing blue cross, he felt a surge of something he could not quite name inside his chest. He thought it might be love.

The next day, Nicole pulled out her day planner and added gold foil stickers to all the dates that she knew the council met. Every Friday beginning that very week—but she didn't put a sticker there. She felt it was too presumptuous to assume they'd want her to start so soon. She was expecting a call from Sara to let her know what the scripture would be for next Tuesday, but one never came. Which was fine with Nicole. She'd see Sara that night at Wednesday fellowship and they could talk then.

Wednesdays were big days at the church. All the members had a potluck they called "fellowship," which was followed by the men's group meeting. The women and children would clean up from the meal and then divide off to do different activities with different age groups of kids. Nicole could go to any activity she wished since she didn't have any kids of her own. Usually, she gravitated to the teens, though Sara continually told her she should spend more time with the youngest children, "to get used to it."

Steve would come in from the field early so he could shower and shave before they left. This week Nicole had made a wild rice dish with roasted apples and butternut squash mixed in. It looked beautiful, although she worried the littler kids wouldn't try it. She hadn't quite mastered the art of Potluck for All Ages. Inevitably someone would just bring a bucket of KFC and put everyone's home-cooked dishes to shame. It was a wonder any of them still cooked at all, but there was a certain amount of pride that went into it. A certain amount of "look what I've done" that came along with any church activity. Look at my cooking, look at my shoes, look at my children and my clothes and my home and family photos and volunteer work. Look at what I have done, not who I am. Because without those things, who were any of them?

The potluck was preceded by a prayer in which the children squirmed and gazed openly at the fried chicken, hoping it wouldn't all be gone by the time they made it through the line.

"Dear Lord," Reverend Grey began, with the same solemn tone he used for sermons, funerals, and weddings. He was a perpetually earnest man. "We give our thanks only to you tonight for this delicious meal that you've allowed us to enjoy."

Steve kept his eyes closed even though it made him feel dizzy. Closing them was part of the rules.

That night the Warbys shared a table with Charity Cole, her husband Andrew, and their three children. The oldest Cole child was Michael, who at the age of fourteen had become sullen and withdrawn from the rest of the family. He still came to church on Sundays and

Wednesdays, but he no longer favored Nicole with wide happy smiles, and Nicole again questioned if children were right for her, because as sweet as the smaller ones were, at some point they stopped making eye contact. His two younger sisters—Lucy, six, and Kaitlin, ten—were still happy to talk to Nicole and show her the latest stuffed animal or Barbie they'd been allowed to bring with as company.

"Hey, Charity." Nicole smiled at the woman who she hoped was her friend.

"How are you doing? Anything new since yesterday?"

"Not really." Nicole was quiet for a moment, trying to decide how to word her thoughts. "This is random, do you know how far the woods go? The ones around the church?"

Charity scrunched up her face. "I try not to think about it. Those woods give me the creeps." She leaned forward and whispered loud enough for the entire table to hear, "You know, sometimes I hear voices out there."

"You mean sometimes you think you hear voices out there," Andrew said. He rolled his eyes and bit into a dinner roll.

Charity blushed and looked down at her plate.

"I thought I heard something out there last night," Nicole offered. "That's why I was wondering how much of them there are."

"Well," Andrew answered around a mouthful of mashed potatoes, "I'd say they stretch back to the highway. I don't know that anyone owns the land."

Now Steve was interested. "That's an awful lot of unowned land. Wonder what that'd go for? Who would you ask?"

"Wouldn't make a good farm, anyways," Andrew said. "I was out there hunting a couple a' years back and it was miserable. Overgrown so's you can barely walk through, not to mention uneven. Ditches so deep they look more like creeks. Came across one path, I can't say where it went. It got dark on me before I realized it."

"I won't let him go back," Charity interrupted. "He was gone the whole day and into the night and when he got back home . . . " Her voice trailed away. "Well, he was shook up pretty bad. Said he kept getting lost."

"Oh, can it, babe. You make it sound like I'm a little kid. It wasn't nothing. She's exaggerating because they scare her, so she wants them to scare me too. I just lost track of time. Nothing too strange about that."

"No, nothing too strange about that," Steve agreed, although he didn't hunt. His father wasn't the hunting type and if he were being honest, Steve wasn't sure he trusted himself not to accidentally shoot his foot with a gun out in the middle of nowhere. He could be absent minded. "Nicole, what'd you mean about hearing voices?"

"I didn't say I heard voices, I said I hear *something*. It's not the same thing."

"Well, what did you hear?"

"Momma, I gotta potty," Lucy said, tugging at her mother's sleeve.

"Well, go then," Charity snapped, brushing her hand away. "You're a big girl now, you can potty by yourself."

"I'm done," Michael muttered. He took his untouched plate to the trash and ambled outside. Nicole watched him through the window as he trudged out to the small playground and sat on one of the swings.

"Kids," Andrew said and laughed, although he wasn't sure what his own joke was.

"There's a house out there, you know," Charity said. "My daddy told me there used to be a little house of some type back in those woods, that's probably what the path you saw goes to, honey."

"Could be. I never heard of any house."

"Daddy said it was a square stone house."

"Sounds more like a fort," Steve said. "Maybe a holdover from some war or another."

"Aren't those usually wooden?" Nicole asked.

"Maybe."

"There aren't any regular houses out there?" Nicole turned back to Charity. "That's a huge bunch of land to be totally empty. Maybe some off-the-grid weirdo set up shop back there."

Charity shrugged and forked broccoli casserole into her mouth. "Like I said, they give me the creeps."

Steve watched his wife settle back into her chair, her mouth puckering into a pout he was more familiar with than he liked to admit. There was something more to the woods. He wondered if he could get to the root of that issue, maybe he could skip out on the whole church council conversation. "When are you going out to the woods?" he asked his wife.

"I'm not. I just come to the church sometimes on my way home from Sara's house. There's no way to get here without being around them."

"I don't know that it's good for you to be hanging around out here by yourself," Steve said.

Nicole glared over at her husband. "You think it's not okay for me to be alone at our own church?"

"I didn't mean it like that."

"What do you mean? That I need an escort?"

"Of course not. Don't be this way." He grinned at Nicole, giving her his best "don't you love me, I'm your cute husband" look. "I just worry about you if you think you're hearing voices in the woods. Who wouldn't worry?"

"I never said it was voices!" Her voice was a little too loud for polite conversation. "I'm not sure why you keep saying I heard voices." She glared at Steve, and Charity worked to suppress a grin. It felt good to see Steve and Nicole fuss at each other, not because she didn't like them, because it made them more like her. She liked Nicole a little better knowing her husband sometimes didn't listen. "Talking about it now, I'm not sure I heard anything. It's just spooky at night, you know?"

"It's creepy all the time," Charity muttered.

Steve realized he couldn't bring up the council here

without alerting the Coles to Nicole's plan, and he wanted to keep the sphere of people who knew about it as small as possible. Contain any potential fallout. The men's meeting was going to begin soon, and he still wasn't sure how to approach Paul Douglas about the idea. He'd wait until it was over, until everyone else was gone. Hopefully he could count on Paul to be discreet, not make a big deal about it.

The men's meeting started as usual, with the members grunting approval of the meal, low single-syllable greetings, the occasional rough laughter as someone made a good-hearted jab about someone's cooking skills. Paul Douglas, husband of Sara Douglas, father of sixteen-year-old twins Rob and Josh Douglas, owner of Douglas Construction, head of the men's group and member of the church council, stood from his chair to call the meeting to order. He was tall and lanky in a way that made you think he probably had trouble finding jeans that fit him. His hair was thin, but still covered his entire head and was no longer any color at all—some sort of mix between blond and grey and tan that just seemed like a lighter and fluffier version of his suntanned scalp. He cracked his knuckles and rolled his neck from side to side as if to work out some sort of tension he'd been holding there his entire life. His eyes were steady and green and slid over the room smooth like paint over primer.

"Good evening, gents. Glad you could join me tonight. It's mighty lonely doing this all on my own." Everyone chuckled at the same joke he told every week because this part was a script, and they were all off book. "Tonight, we have some old business, some new business, and some regular old scripture business. Before we begin, does anyone have any news they need to report?"

The room stayed silent, which was good. No one wanted extra business cluttering up the agenda, making them late. Everyone had a Styrofoam cup of plain black coffee in front of them and most took this opportunity to have a sip.

"Sounds good. Let's get into the pancake breakfast details."

Steve Warby, father to no one, husband to Nicole, stayed quiet throughout the meeting. He practiced talking to Paul, something he'd done very little of since he'd known him. Something he had mostly avoided when it got right down to it. Not because he didn't like him—everyone liked Paul—because Steve felt he knew his place. Paul was simply above him, and he was okay with that. Nicole wasn't. Nicole was ambitious in a way maybe Steve just wasn't. And maybe she couldn't finish a project for the life of her, but damned if she didn't come up with projects to do. Damned if she didn't just love planning something new to not finish.

After the meeting, Paul stayed behind, gathering his papers, notes, and Bible—sliding them all into something not quite like a briefcase. Steve's stomach flipped a little as he approached him. He cleared his throat.

"Uh, Paul?"

"Hey there, Steve, how's it coming out there?"

"Oh, it's good. Can't complain."

"Well that's real good to hear, friend." Paul patted him on the shoulder as he moved past him toward the door.

"Oh, actually, Paul, I needed to say something. I mean, talk to you. If you have a minute."

Paul paused and Steve watched his back as he rolled his neck to either side. Even so, his voice was clear and pleasant as he said, "Sure thing, Steve-o. What's on your mind?"

"Well, not so much my mind as my wife's. As Nicole's. You see, she's got this idea in her head that she wants to be on the church council and asked me to bring it up to you." Steve's vision slid to the ground and found a small stain to linger on as he spoke. He wondered what it was.

"That's . . . " Paul's voice trailed off and he sounded uncertain. "The thing is, those things are usually done by invitation. I know you folks are still newer to the church, you wouldn't know, so it's not a problem. People don't just ask to be on council."

"Oh, yep. Yeah. That does make sense." Steve thought the stain could have been grape juice.

Paul's voice gained speed as the confidence seeped back into it. "I don't mind bringing it to the pastor. I don't mind one bit."

"No, that's fine. No need to bother Reverend Grey about it. I don't want to cause a fuss. Just, gosh, Paul, you know how the ladies can be, when they get an idea, they don't want to let it go. I had to bring it up or else I'd never hear the end, you know what I mean?" He added a short chuckle to prove how silly it all was.

"Oh, certainly. I do understand. Sara gets a mind to serve us some new fancy dinners some nights and there's no convincing her no one wants to try out a chicken piccata on a Tuesday, but there we are, trying it anyway."

"Exactly, this is just Nicole's chicken piccata."

"Say, what made her decide on the council?" Paul asked.

"I'm not sure, she just got a wild notion because of whatever they were talking about in women's group this week. Something about women being prophets."

Paul laughed. "Does she think she's a prophet now?"

"No, no, nothing that serious. She just thought you guys might like having a woman on council. A different perspective, I guess."

"Is she unhappy with the perspectives on the council now?" Paul asked, still smiling. Still friendly. But a different edge to his tone.

"Of course not. She's just still looking for her place here in Lilin, trying to figure where she belongs in all this."

"I getcha. Just her own little chicken piccata."

"Absolutely," Steve said. "Well, thanks for taking the time, I don't want to keep you. Have a good night."

"You too."

Steve cursed himself as he walked out to the car. He

knew Nicole would be waiting for him out there. Too much socialization started to wear on her.

"How did it go?" she asked him as soon as he'd closed the door.

"I'm real sorry, honey, he said that the council was by invitation only. People didn't get to ask, they have to be asked."

"Oh." She didn't say anything else and Steve didn't want to press the issue, so he started the car and pointed it toward home.

Once inside, Nicole changed and headed straight to bed. Steve pulled out a Budweiser from the fridge and sat down at the kitchen table. He chose a point on the wall and stared, thinking of nothing, wanting nothing.

CHAPTER 3

ON SUNDAY MORNING Steve would make breakfast, less because he wanted to do something nice and more because he knew Nicole would sleep until she only had enough time to dress and get to church. And he liked breakfast. It was his favorite meal of the week. And if he made bacon, he knew she would get out of bed to eat it with him. Nicole had been in a mood since Wednesday, and he needed to do something to bring her out of it before things got worse. And they could get worse. Steve had seen them worse. He'd seen her not leave her bed for a week. He'd seen her dirty, smelling unwashed and feral. Her hair would tangle and she'd end up cutting it short just to get the knots out. He'd seen her worse and was in no mood to deal with that at the moment.

He pushed the bedroom door open and tried to sound cheerful. "Honey, I made some breakfast. You want to come out and have some coffee with me?"

"Is there bacon?" she asked.

"Absolutely. Then after, we'll get cleaned up for church, right?"

"Church. Yeah, that's fine. We can go to church."

Steve was worried about her. And Nicole guessed he had reason to worry. Or, at least, she'd given him reason in the past. This didn't feel the same. But did it ever feel the same? Was the way things were ever in line with the way things are? All Nicole knew for sure was that her purpose here seemed a little less certain than it had on

Wednesday morning. Yet that didn't mean she had no purpose. Just that God hadn't shown it to her. It was entirely possible that she would live to be 300 years old and only then find meaning in this world. The thought brought her enough comfort to get out of bed and eat bacon with Steve.

"So, how are you feeling?" Steve asked. He was casual. This was a question that meant nothing.

"Just a little off. I think I might have an inner ear thing."

"Oh." This reply was unexpected. Off-script.

"Yeah, I felt a little dizzy last night. Sort of nauseous. Coffee will help." She grinned, wide and toothless, and Steve wanted to believe that sweet face.

"Maybe you should see a doctor on Monday. If the ear's not any better."

"I agree. I don't think I should wait too long. It seems like it might be getting smaller in there. If I wait too long, they won't be able to see inside." She said all this as if it were perfectly reasonable.

"Smaller?"

"Swollen."

They sank into a bloated silence. The sun was shining and Steve wished he could be out in it. The heat bleaching his mind until he didn't have to think about his wife's incredible shrinking ear or how nonchalantly she brought it up.

It was Nicole that broke the silence. Always Nicole. "I want you to know, I still plan to do more at the church. I didn't give up."

"Honey, I think you already do plenty. I just want you to be happy."

"I want that too."

The room hummed with electricity. Nicole could hear it a little too distinctly. Not just the fridge motor, but the lights and coffee maker as well. Everything plugged into an outlet. It was all softly screaming at her.

Her ear was closing, and it felt like a relief. At least she wouldn't hear all that electricity.

"You should probably get dressed," Steve suggested. He was such a helper.

"You're exactly right." Nicole smiled at him, and the smile exhausted her.

The church sanctuary didn't have stained glass windows. Nicole used to think this was odd, and maybe she still did, now at least she appreciated it. She could see outside to the nature surrounding the building. Usually, it made her feel connected to the world. Today, it made her feel claustrophobic. Something was no longer right. She couldn't pinpoint what it was or how it had changed, but she was no longer comforted in the small church by the woods.

Her ears were ringing constantly now. She pressed her hand against the right ear and used her palm to create a gentle suction, trying to adjust the pressure. After a few seconds Nicole felt a tickling sensation, a shiver raced through her body, and she promptly poked her pointer finger inside. There was a hard little ball in the cup of her ear, and she swept it out and peered curiously at her new treasure.

A tiny pill bug looked back at her. Revolted, she flicked it away and sheepishly glanced around the room to see if anyone had noticed. The ringing was gone, but now her hearing was even more muffled. Tentatively she pushed her finger back inside. There was nothing there, despite that the canal seemed smaller than before, as if it was closing itself off from further intrusion.

"Ears don't do that," she muttered, trying to be Steve.

"What's that?" Steve asked. He didn't look at her.

"Nothing," she hissed.

A long and sudden chord from the organ signaled that

they should stand, and they did. Kaitlin Cole walked down the center aisle first, a long gold candlelighter held tight in her small hands. She lit the two white taper candles set up on the altar at the head of the sanctuary and scurried a bit too fast back down the aisle to her mother, who was undoubtedly waiting for her on the other side of the double doors. Next the choir walked in, double-file—women on the right, men on the left. The candles on the altar felt obscene. Heat flooded Nicole's face. Why did they have an altar at all?

Reverend Grey entered last, his face emotionless, his gaze steady. Nicole tried to remember a time she saw him smiling and immediately hated herself for being so critical. Of course he smiled. Of course he did. It was just so hot in here. The candles made it hotter than it should be.

"Good morning," he said to the congregation—and he smiled as he said it.

"Good morning," the congregation repeated—Nicole could not smile in return. Her stomach did a tiny flip, and she swallowed a wave of nausea. Now there was an ice-cold ball sitting inside her stomach. It was the deepest circle of Hell. The betrayer was in that ice.

The choir sang, they said a prayer, the choir sang, there was a children's sermon—something about temptation. Nicole stood and sat when everyone did, but she couldn't bring herself to mouth the words of the songs. She was afraid that the moment she opened her mouth a swarm of little bugs would escape. She could feel them just behind her teeth, moving like a sentient wave over her tongue.

Reverend Grey stood at the pulpit and stared out at them. He looked quietly for a long time until people started to shift uncomfortably, a few even chuckled, their nerves spilling out as harsh, staccato sounds.

Finally, he took a long breath and let it whoosh out directly onto the tiny black microphone.

"There are witches in the woods." His voice was hard. There was no argument here. No debate or exceptions. He was not taking questions today.

"There are witches in the woods." Louder this time.

"But do these witches also come out of the woods?" His gaze did not waver. "Today I will begin reading to you from Ephesians, chapter five, verses twenty-two through twenty-four. Feel free to follow along in your Bibles. 'Wives, submit yourselves to your own husbands as you do to the Lord. For the husband is the head of the wife as Christ is the head of the church, his body, of which he is the Savior. Now as the church submits to Christ, so also wives should submit to their husbands in everything.'

"What does it mean, my friends? What is it, first, to submit to God? Does it mean that we question God? That we debate Him? NO!"

The last word was loud enough to make the sound system protest.

Reverend Grey let it settle over them before he continued. "It means, very simply, very plainly, we do not compromise with God. He is the first and final word. You do not listen to your friends if they go against what God has commanded.

"And this is what it is for wives to submit to your husbands.

"You must fully submit, with your whole being. If you submit to your husband in actions, yet in your mind you still doubt him—that is not submission! You must trust—fully trust—in your husband to make the right choices.

"And husbands, what does this mean for you? To be the leader of your home? Does it mean whatever you wish is your wife's command? No! It means that you must be in constant communion with God. You must know and speak and lead by what God commands. A man who does not know God cannot lead his family."

He paused here and surveyed the congregation, and Nicole did the same. The faces around her nodded in agreement. The pill bugs in her mouth threatened to escape at the corners of her lips, and she locked her teeth together hard and swallowed. The swarm moved halfway down her throat and then crawled slowly back into her mouth. The sensation made her want to cough, but she didn't dare.

"If we are truly to give ourselves to God, we must respect and honor the authority that He has put into place for us. We must trust that He knows what is right. When He placed man at the head of the household, He did so with His own infallible wisdom. Who are we to doubt this?

"And I know you—I know you in your arrogance. You are asking me, 'Reverend Grey, doesn't submission make me weak? Reverend Grey, I am a strong modern woman—how can you tell me to submit?'

"Let me ask you this—Was Jesus weak? Are you to say that Jesus Christ, son of God, was weak? NO! Did he not submit himself to the will of God? In fact, it takes a person who is spiritually strong to submit. You cannot submit, truly submit, if you are not strong in faith and your relationship with God." He let that settle upon them for a few long seconds before continuing.

"Men of my flock, are your wives strong in faith? Are they spiritually strong? Or are they strong in resistance? Do they excel in stubborn pride? There are witches in the woods, and they would hex your relationships. They would infiltrate your homes, this very church, and put a spell on your wives to make them believe that they must be defiant in order to be equal. That equality means arguing and turning away from the roles that God has given us. That God has blessed us with! How glorious to be able to move in this world knowing exactly the role you are born to fill, exactly how you should live. God has given us this certainty! Why would we deny He who has given us everything?

"Remember that in Samuel it is written that rebellion is as the sin of witchcraft, and stubbornness is as iniquity and idolatry. My children, I love you all as any parent would. Which means being stern when needed. I have felt a cloud moving over my congregation. I have prayed on it for weeks. Too many of you have strayed from the strong spiritually faithful paths that God has laid out for you. I have asked God what can be done. And his answer to me was loud and clear—we must rid the witches from our midst."

Steve's eyes cut over to Nicole, he couldn't tell what she was thinking. All her concentration was on the bugs. The words of Reverend Grey slid through her mind like water.

"We must break the curses and bring harmony back to our homes."

Nicole stood up.

"There are witches in the woods, and I mean to cast them out."

Steve grabbed at her hand, but she yanked it away. Stepping into the center aisle of the sanctuary, she took two steps forward before falling to her knees and retching onto the soft green carpet. Thick black mud gushed from her mouth. Tendrils of spit and mucus clung to her lips and made slow trails down to the floor. The last thing Nicole heard before fainting into her vomit was the sound of the reverend's voice, "They are among us."

Steve knelt by his wife, pulled her face out of the puddle, and tried to suppress a gag. Dark clots were smeared from her mouth to her hairline. It looked like she'd eaten a bag of gardening soil. He squinted at the mound, saw things wriggling in there, and had to look away.

"Nicole, honey, wake up."

He leaned his ear down to her mouth to check for breathing.

"Is she okay?" It was Paul Douglas.

"I don't know," Steve shouted, his voice sounding much louder and more panicked than he would have liked.

"Calm down, Steve, it's going to be okay." Paul spoke with confidence, and Steve believed him because he didn't have any other choice. It had to be okay. He felt the soft whisper of Nicole's breath against his cheek—the sweetest thing he'd ever felt.

"She's breathing," Steve told the room. The room did not respond.

"That's real good," Paul said. "Let's get her up outta this. Can you lift her?"

"Yeah, of course." Steve tried to scoop her up, but she was all limp dead weight and he let her slip back down into her puke again. A soft wail came out of his mouth without permission.

"Okay, no problem," Paul told him. "I'll get her ankles and you get up under her arms. We can take her out to . . . " His voice trailed, and Steve understood that Paul had no real idea what to do. He was just in charge out of habit, not experience or skill.

Steve had Nicole's head in his lap now and he patted her cheek, hot and slick with bile, sweat, and fever. Her lips twitched at the corners like a smile she wanted to suppress.

"Nicole?" he whispered, pleading.

"Are we finished?" she whispered back to him, eyes still closed. "Can we go now?"

"She's coming around, let's give her room," Paul said, although there was no need. Everyone was still in their seats. Reverend Grey was still at the pulpit. Only Nicole and the two men had moved.

"Wake up," Steve said.

"Wake up," Nicole mimicked.

"Nicole?"

"Nicole?"

"Are you with us?"

"Are you with us?"

A long silence. Minutes or maybe only seconds ticked away, and Steve was afraid to breathe. Nicole's eyes opened one after the other. First right, then left. Which wasn't so bad, except then she started blinking the same way. Right eye closed, left eye closed. Right eye open, left eye open. Over and over.

"Why's she doing that?" Paul asked. Was that fear somewhere in his voice?

"Wake up." Nicole's voice was a hushed and urgent whisper. "Wake up, wake up, wake up wake upwakeup." The inside of her mouth was unnaturally dark. Steve saw a tiny pill bug scurry out and up her cheek.

"Is she . . . Does she have some sort of sickness?"

Steve didn't answer because he didn't know.

Both eyes popped open like a baby doll—no more blinking, stuttered or otherwise.

"Steve?" she asked.

The room had been holding its breath and now it whooshed out with enough force to take out the clear and distinctly unstained glass of the windows. Except it didn't. The windows held and the room was just a room now—with all the sounds and shuffles and sniffles that you never notice until they disappear.

"I'm right here."

"I need to get out of here."

"Can you stand up, maybe . . . maybe go to the bathroom?"

Nicole moved to her knees and swiped the back of her left hand against the muddy smears on her face. She looked at her hand, considered what she saw—then, fast as a snake, her tongue darted out and licked it.

"She's hexed."

Steve looked up to see who had spoken. It was Reverend Grey, no longer at the pulpit. He stood in front of them now, his shoes at the edge of the chunky pile of dirt clods and mud Nicole had retched into existence.

"I'm sorry," Nicole whimpered. "I tried to keep it in." She lowered her face, her arms wide, fingers splayed, as if she were bowing before Reverend Grey. She lapped the sickness from the floor back into her mouth, her eyes raised to the reverend. Tears oozed down her cheeks trying to make paths in the crusted filth. "I take it back."

"Stop it!" Steve cried. He yanked her shoulders, and she flew into him, the back of her head smashing his chin. "Somebody, please, call an ambulance. She's sick, she's sick." He started to blubber, snot and tears mixing as he lost the last of his control and that childlike fear of helplessness overtook him.

It was Sara Douglas who finally pulled her cell phone from her purse and called 911. Donna Marin rushed down from the choir, pulled off her robe, and laid it over the vomit because out of sight, out of mind (mouth). Reverend Grey stood unnaturally tall over the couple who was crying and gagging together on the floor, one trying to consume and the other trying to stop her.

"How can we deny the Devil when we see him so plainly?"

Nicole howled and clawed, trying to get back to the puke, her fingers worming under the robe. She raked at it with her nails and sucked at whatever lodged itself beneath them. Steve tried to pin her arms. He looked at Paul for help and Paul looked away. No more help today.

When the ambulance arrived, they had to restrain and sedate Nicole with droperidol in order to get her into the rig. Steve, looking somehow smaller than he had earlier that day, got in his car and followed the ambulance as it rode away from the small church next to the woods, leaving the rest of the congregation behind with nothing except confusion, fear, and a pile of vomit.

Charity Cole stood at the edge of the parking lot looking out into the woods. Nicole had asked her about these woods only a few days ago. Asked her if anything about them seemed wrong. And things certainly did seem wrong. If she unfocused her eyes and looked the way you do at a Magic Eye, she thought she could see movement out there. Not the normal branches bouncing with squirrels, something else. A shimmer of slow, slow movement—something that didn't want to be seen. Sounds trying not to be heard.

"I guess we'll need to find someone else to read the verse this week," Sara said, coming up next to Charity.

"Don't be cute."

"I was being practical."

"Don't be that either. There's nothing at all practical about what just happened," Charity said.

"Paul said he's heard about people eating the wrong stuff, although it seems like we'd have noticed before this."

"I don't think that's it."

"I don't either."

They stood together quietly, each looking into the woods. Each seeing something just a little bit different.

Nicole was in a hospital gown now, Steve was still dressed in his filthy church clothes. He smelled sour and his shirt felt crispy like a dried-up hunk of phlegm. He'd tried talking to his wife, but she was groggy or didn't want to talk to him or both. It was probably best just to let her be still for a while. They had the rest of their lives to have these conversations.

Reverend Grey arrived two hours later, his face still stern. Steve wanted him to smile, to assure him. He was left wanting.

"I am sorry that this has happened, Mr. Warby."

Mister? Where had the formality come from? "I—you know me, Reverend. I'm just Steve."

"I don't want to delay this any longer. I fear your wife needs intervention."

"She's sick."

"Have you noticed anything strange about your wife lately?"

One man's strange was another man's baseline. "No, not really." Then he corrected, "Outside of today, of course."

"Mr. Warby, Paul Douglas told me something that has

me deeply troubled. He told me your wife has asked to join our church council. That she went so far as to coerce you to speak on her behalf." The reverend looked angry, and Steve felt like a child being called to the principal's office. Except, he reminded himself, he'd done nothing wrong.

"Sir, that did happen. But I don't think it's cause for concern. Nicole's just looking for a place to belong."

"Let me ask you a few questions. Is your wife a good homemaker?"

"Ah, well." Steve paused to think. "I guess that's relative. She does real good sometimes. In phases, I'd say."

"I see. And does she show ambition outside of the home?"

"I'm not sure I understand."

"Then let me be plain. I believe your wife is hexed."

Steve laughed. He didn't mean to, it leapt out of him too suddenly to hold it back. "Reverend, I'm sorry, that's nutty. Nicole's sick right now. But that's not her. Today wasn't her. She gets a little down every now and then, yeah. And she tries too hard sometimes and maybe not hard enough others, that's Nicole. That's just her."

"Here is what I have seen, Mr. Warby. Your wife has tried to take a place in God's holy house that is reserved for men, because God has designated it to be so."

"Neither of us really knew that."

"She is not accepting the role she was born to play and instead boldly reaching for ones that she could not possibly fill. She is prone to bouts of sadness. She is childless—"

"Well, now—"

"A witch's curse can cause pain in the ribs and stomach; it eats away at you. You saw what came out of her today. I don't think I need to explain more on that subject. I want you to ask yourself, Mr. Warby, is your wife virtuous and submissive? Or is she bold, stubborn, and arrogant? Does she bow to your will, or does she attempt to make you bend?"

"Reverend Grey, I don't mean any disrespect, but we've

never really been those sort of people." Steve had reached the end of the things he could tolerate for any given day—especially a Sunday. "I wouldn't call her submissive, I don't ask her to be. That's not how we operate."

"You assume to know how to better 'operate' than God?"

"I think you need to leave for now, Reverend. My wife is sick."

Reverend Grey stood still, and Steve feared that he might have to ask him to leave for a second time, which somehow seemed much more disrespectful. For a day that started with bacon, it was turning out to be pretty lousy.

"I understand. But please, think on what I've told you today. The signs are there. It is not just your wife. I fear for many in our flock." He left without another word and Steve could have almost believed it was altogether a dream. Surely no grown man had just come to his wife's hospital room and accused her of being hexed by a witch. That didn't happen.

"I don't feel like a witch," Nicole whispered.

"Well, I don't think he was calling you a witch." Steve smiled. He walked over to his wife and kissed her forehead. "He's just concerned, that's all. We're all concerned."

"I think I feel a little bit better."

"That's a good thing."

There was a question in the air. It floated in front of Steve like smoke. "Hun, I don't want to make you feel bad all over again, it's only, I know the doctors are going to be asking." He took a deep breath. "What were you doing eating all that dirt?"

"I never ate any dirt, Steve. That's just the thing. I wouldn't do that. It was just inside of me."

"Sure, but things don't get inside of us, not things like that, without a little help."

"Not this time. This time it grew there. It just . . . it grew there."

Steve decided to let the subject die. He didn't want to upset her. Didn't want to risk another episode like earlier.

There was no more dirt inside Nicole Warby. Whatever she'd ingested had entirely evacuated the premises. Although she still insisted to everyone she hadn't ingested anything more harmful than bacon and coffee.

A doctor named Glen Turley visited the room and Steve immediately liked him. He was very old and bald, and something about that felt comforting. Someone so old would know what to do. He had experience, he'd seen it all, he'd seen something like this a million times before and he would help. "Is there any way dirt like that can get inside someone without eating it?" Steve asked the doctor.

"Not in the amounts you described. We breathe in dust and particles every day, this isn't the same thing."

"What do we do?"

"I'm going to recommend Nicole see a therapist here in the clinic. That might help us figure out what happened today."

Steve took the business card handed to him, but knew they'd never call the therapist. Therapy cost money, and farms didn't exactly come with stellar health insurance. Nicole wasn't a danger to herself—this was debatable—or others—this was also debatable, according to the bruise on Steve's chin. She didn't have a fever, and other than seeming disoriented (perhaps a bit dehydrated), there was nothing medically wrong with Nicole Warby. And it was time to go home. The old doctor had failed Steve and he felt betrayed. It was the theme of his day. It seemed everyone he'd ever known had betrayed him on this particular Sunday and suddenly he had the very strong urge to finally call his mother. A mother was exactly what this situation needed. Unfortunately for Mrs. Warby, this urge ebbed almost immediately. The clean florescence of the hospital stole the warm desire for family right out of his heart and replaced it with the familiar need to look at a wall and feel nothing.

Their home was dark when they arrived.

"I need to have a shower," Steve said. "Are you okay out here?"

"Of course."

She waited for the bathroom door to close and the water to start before she even sat down on the couch. The bugs were gone now, but her ear was still too small. The words of Reverend Grey came back to haunt her. She was not a good homemaker, not fulfilling her role. If not cleaning the baseboards had made her sick, then she supposed she should start cleaning them. Maybe the purpose she'd been searching for wasn't somewhere else, in an outside club or organization, perhaps it was in her home. She'd start tomorrow.

The idea of attending the women's group on Tuesday made her nervous. She'd embarrassed herself at church. For all she knew they wouldn't let her in the front door. *No Witches Allowed.*

A silly thought. She was no witch. In fact, Nicole didn't think she believed in witches, and she suspected the other women didn't either. She'd be interested to hear what they had to say about today's sermon. From what she remembered, she suspected the women might be suspicious of that kind of talk. Donna was definitely not a submissive wife. Although her home was admittedly cleaner than Nicole's.

Once he was clean, the events of the day really didn't seem so bad to Steve. The human brain had a remarkable ability to release trauma. It held no true memory of physical pain. Once it was over, it seemed like it couldn't have possibly been as agonizing. His wife was going to be just fine. So maybe she'd accidentally eaten a little dirt. These things happen.

On the other hand, maybe it was a hex.

He chuckled at the idea. And then he didn't. Because Nicole had been off lately. And she wasn't exactly what a person might call agreeable. And what kind of non-hexed person ate dirt? These things didn't happen.

CHAPTER 4

ON TUESDAY EVENING Steve drove Nicole over to the Douglas house himself. He was nervous she might not really go, and he wanted to keep an eye on her as much as possible. He didn't like the idea of her sneaking off and finding a pile of mulch to snack on instead of Bible study.

Nicole insisted he not walk her to the door, so he simply kissed her cheek and watched her as she traipsed up the driveway, her sneakers crunching in gravel. She hugged herself tight and Steve could tell she was nervous.

"I love you," he called to her.

Nicole only waved him away, both annoyed and thankful for her new babysitter. He stayed until he saw Sara greet her at the door before backing carefully away from the house and pointing his truck in the direction of home.

"Nicole!" Sara cried. "I didn't think you'd be up to visiting today. Are you doing better?"

"I feel much better, honestly. I'm so ashamed about Sunday. I don't know what got into me."

"It was dirt, darling," Donna said. She was a little bitter about having to clean it up. Although she was definitely getting the new choir robe she wanted because her old one was completely ruined.

Nicole laughed. "You know, everyone says that, but I don't think it was dirt. It must have been something else that just looked like dirt. Chocolate cake."

"Did you eat any chocolate cake?" Charity asked.

"No, well, not that I remember. Who really knows what they eat in a day."

The women exchanged glances. Donna not only knew what she ate in a day, but how many calories, fat grams, and carbohydrates each item contained. She wasn't accidentally eating anything. The whole idea offended her almost as much as cleaning up a pile of regurgitated dirt and having someone try to tell her it was chocolate.

"Well, I think we should get started right away tonight," Sara said. "I have some exciting news." She paused for dramatic effect. "Reverend Grey has graciously given us new women's Bible study materials. I haven't had much time to look through it yet, but I think it's going to be fantastic."

"What's it about?" Nicole asked.

"Let's all find out together." Sara passed out thin booklets as well as much thicker spiral-bound journal-sized books to each woman. "We can start right on page one. Since no one had a chance to prepare, I'll go ahead and just lead us tonight. Because honestly, I'm just so thrilled for the first part here. Just check out the thicker book, ladies."

The women flipped through with decidedly less enthusiasm than Sara thought appropriate.

"It's a planner?" Charity asked.

"Well, sort of," Sara said. "It's a homemaking planner! Each month has checklists and stuff to help you maintain your household. There are cleaning schedules, and places to write notes on each week's sermons. Look at it."

"I think it's great," Nicole chimed in. "I've been thinking I need to put more effort into my home."

"I think I already know how to wash my laundry, but I guess it doesn't hurt anything," Donna said, more to herself than the room.

Everyone was quiet then. Sara wasn't pleased with the reaction and wasn't trying to hide it. The only person excited about it was the crazy one.

“It also has some cleaning recipes,” Charity said.

“What’s a cleaning recipe?” Donna asked.

“For cleaning solutions. Natural ones. That’s pretty nice.”

Sara smiled at Charity. “Well, our first verse and study session is actually a tie-in to last week’s sermon about submissiveness in a Christian marriage.”

“Really?” Nicole asked. “I kind of figured we wouldn’t be interested in that.”

“Why wouldn’t we be interested?” Sara asked, her tone sharp.

“Because, well, we were just talking about Deborah and a woman’s role as a leader last week. I thought we sort of agreed that submission wasn’t what we were here for, as the female leadership of our church.”

“And that attitude is exactly the problem. You’re making a presumption that you know best—better than what is clearly spelled out for us in the Good Book.”

“I wasn’t implying that.”

“Then why don’t you take a submissive role right now and actually listen to the lesson for once, Nicole.” Sara’s words bit harder than usual, and Nicole’s eyes stung. She didn’t reply, only looked down at her new Bible study book and pretended to read a recipe for lemon cutting board cleanser.

“Now, let me begin, if that’s okay. You can open your booklets, there are places for you to take notes.” The women rummaged briefly in their purses for ink pens.

Sara cleared her throat. “‘In Colossians 3:18, it says that wives should submit to their husbands, as is fitting the Lord. Sounds pretty simple, right?’”

Charity nodded her head and took a note, but for the life of her Nicole couldn’t figure out what she would be writing. They hadn’t said anything yet.

“‘The Greek word Paul uses here is a military term meaning to put oneself in rank under another. It does not mean to be a slave. Every time God commands wives in the

Bible, it is to say that she should be submissive to her husband. And that he in turn should be submissive to God. When we follow the plan that God has presented us, our homes will be in harmony.'"

Sara stopped here and looked at the other women in the room. Apparently, it was time for a response. Nicole knew she shouldn't speak yet. She needed to see what the other ladies thought first. She needed to get their opinions on what they'd heard.

Donna was the brave one. "I get the idea. I just feel like it's too easy to abuse. If your husband always gets the last word, what's going to stop him from using it to have whatever he wants all the time?"

"God," Sara replied simply. "If your husband is righteous then he is going to use his authority for good. It's like it said, the word means like military authority. In the military they aren't making selfish decisions."

Nicole chewed the insides of her cheeks.

"What if I hate Chinese food, but my husband loves it, so he keeps making us go there for dinner?" Charity asked.

"What makes you think it's not in your best interest? Maybe he's doing that to lead you to appreciate different cultures or foods. The same way you make your kids eat carrots. Because as the parent, you know better." Sara smiled. She was enjoying this new version of Bible study, where she always knew the correct answer because the correct answer was always "God." If you simply have faith, then you have nothing to worry about. And if you don't have faith, you should be trying harder.

"I trust my husband, but there are some things I know better than he does," Donna said.

Sara sighed. "Sure, of course. That's where your husband must be wise enough to listen to you. None of this is saying you never share an opinion. It's exactly like a judge. He listens to all the important facts then decides."

"Juries decide," Nicole blurted out before she could stop herself.

"Not in the Bible, sister," Sara corrected.

"Okay, so what's the end goal here?" Donna asked. "What's the long game? Why is this suddenly an issue for us that Reverend Grey thinks we need to change our whole lives?"

"Reverend Grey believes—because God has instructed him—that the church is pulling away from God. He must do everything within his power to stop that. We need to correct course in our lives. The reverend's long game is our eternal souls, which he has been charged by God to save." Sara sounded so earnest.

"What's it got to do with witches?" Nicole asked.

Sara didn't have an immediate answer and the room went still.

"Are the witches a metaphor?" Charity asked.

"I'm not sure," Sara sighed.

"I don't think it's a metaphor, and that worries me," Donna said.

"All I know for sure is, this is what the council has asked us to do. And I think we should do it. And I think we shouldn't make a fuss." Sara's face held all the sternness but none of the bite. In her eyes, Nicole saw her own mother—pleading with her not to be a problem. Not because it was right, because it was expected.

Steve was waiting outside when Nicole came out of Sara's.

"How did it go?" he asked.

"A little bizarre. The church council gave us new Bible study materials. It's a day planner, which is kind of nice, only the focus of the lesson was the same as the last sermon, all about submissive wives."

Steve considered this as he drove. The church council always met on Saturday, which meant they made this plan before the puking incident on Sunday, but after his conversation with Paul on Wednesday. He couldn't stop thinking this was somehow about him and Nicole. The idea was wildly paranoid—knew it was—they could have been planning this for months.

He'd left the porch light on when he left, and its yellow glow guided him up the long driveway. Nicole was out and in the house almost before he'd put the truck in park. She flicked on every light switch she passed, and Steve followed the trail of wasted electricity into the kitchen.

"I don't feel comfortable with all this submissive witch business. If nothing else, it's spooky. I knew when we joined this church it was a little bit . . . small town. I didn't think it was puritanical," Nicole said.

"I don't think that's fair. The people in this church have been really good to us. I like it there."

"Well, sure, no one's asking you to submit to me." She meant for it to sound like a joke, but her voice was a tad too shrill.

"Look, I'm not asking for anything to change between us. So why don't we just nod along while we're there and I bet eventually this stuff will go away." He was saying what he wanted to believe.

"Do you think it's because I asked to be on the council?"

"I don't know." Steve definitely believed it was because she asked to be on the council.

"I don't feel right about all this."

"Okay, well, maybe you should pray about it. Spend some time talking to God, give it to Him and see how you feel." He knew it was the right answer, yet it still felt wrong.

"That solution normally sounds real nice, but right now it feels plain ominous."

"Maybe that's the problem right there. If the right thing feels wrong, maybe that should tell you something. Maybe you're going the wrong way." Steve was excited. He thought he was on to something now. The church was right. And if the church felt wrong, it must be them who was wrong. It was like a word problem.

"I guess this is one of those times I should practice submitting, right? If you think I should pray about it, then that's what I'll do." The shrill in her voice had taken on a certain edge that made Steve nervous. It conjured the image of a woman who felt so guilty about her failed garden that she ate the dirt to erase the evidence. A woman so lost she grasped at every whim like a life preserver and every admonishment like a death sentence.

"I just want us to be happy. I want to leave in the morning for the field and come back in the evening to a hot meal and a clean house. I'm not asking you to make holistic lemon floor cleaner—"

"That's not what holistic means."

"And that isn't the point! I'm trying to build a life here. A life I thought you wanted. A simple life. A good life. One where we do things for each other because they make us happy, not because we're keeping up with the Joneses."

"I know, you don't want to be your father. You don't want me to be your mother. And I'm not. I know I'm not her. But I also don't know who I am. I'm afraid I'm no one, Steve." She didn't tell him that when she looked in the mirror her reflection was fading, like she was ebbing away from existence altogether.

"I don't like it when you talk like that."

"Does that mean I should stop because my husband hath spoken?"

"Don't do this. Don't hurt me because you're afraid. All I'm asking is for you to take some time, pray on it."

"I know. You're right."

He couldn't tell if she was still attacking or if she'd given in. The two sounded eerily similar coming from her. When he came to bed only an hour later, Nicole was already there, her eyes closed, her hands clasped over her chest as if in prayer. And still, he didn't know.

Nicole waited until Steve's deep breathing gave way to long snoring then slipped out of bed like a cat. She leaned against the walls to avoid the worn and creaky boards in the middle of the hallway. She slithered down the staircase to the front door and out into the darkness. The days here were hot as fire, but the nights still felt cool. The humidity lingered. It never lifted until suddenly one day in the fall—*poof*! It would disappear so fast you wouldn't notice until a week or two later when you were reaching for a jacket before you headed out and then there it'd be.

She worried for a moment that the car would wake her husband, but decided that if it did, oh well. She'd already be gone by then.

The car already knew the way to the church. In fact, all it knew was the church and the grocery store. She tried the doors without much hope and found them locked. That was fine. She didn't want inside, and it wasn't until she couldn't get in that she realized it. She wanted out there—she wanted to be in the woods. And the woods were happy to have her.

Her steps were slow, shuffling through the floor of decayed leaves and new growth. A thousand tiny maple trees reached up from the ground searching for room. A thousand little babies that couldn't live. There were still fireflies, but they were slow and lazy. She made out the shape of a fallen tree ahead and she only briefly worried there might be a snake before walking toward it. She was here to pray. If God wanted her to be bitten by a snake, she would be.

The bark was rough in parts and smooth in others. Nicole straddled the tree and laid face down on it, her cheek nestled into a patch of moss. Smells of death and life mingled together in the woods creating a special new kind of beauty.

"God, tell me what to do. Make me good."

Nicole held her breath and waited. There were soft little footsteps around her—deer or raccoons or children.

Then there was a voice. Or maybe a rustle. Something like the sound of wind chimes came in on a low breeze. Nicole thought about the things beneath her—the buried things existing in the in-between places. There was an art to burying your secrets. If you go too deep it's obvious, everyone expects it to be there. Too shallow and a tourist trips over it. You had to get it just right. You had to find the sweet spot.

Was there a voice? Nicole tried to ignore the sounds. Things people said out loud were only wishes. The truth was something else. One of the in-betweens. Or maybe it was listening to the voices and sorting out reality from wishes.

Except this voice only said her name—not much to sort. Did the voice wish for her or was she its reality?

Nicole raised herself off the log and looked around the woods. She was too deep to see the bold LED cross from the church and she was surprised to realize she was actually glad. Seeing the woods as they were now, soft and damp, made the idea of that white-blue light of the cross seem vulgar. Did the creatures of the forest think it was garish? Did they care?

Her sight adjusted to the dark. The moon was half full, however that didn't account for all the light. No, the plants seemed to be illuminated from the inside. Those green little cells she'd diagrammed in grade school were more alive than ever. Except there was a darker patch right ahead of her and she shuffled over to it, her curiosity spiked.

It was a pair of shoes. Women's dress shoes with a low chunky heel and a thick strap over the top like a Mary Jane. The toe was rounded and wide. The entire shoe was black, except not really. Not really because there was a layer of thick green moss growing over them. There they sat, side by side on display. The matte leather was clean and fresh—all except, of course, for the moss.

Nicole stood up and backed away from the shoes. They shouldn't be there; they were not right. This was not the place where they belonged. This was not the time for these shoes. She'd found the clues out of order; she was ruining everything.

Then it was upon her, the voice that had wished for her name. It slithered in behind and laced itself along her limbs and torso. Nicole considered struggling for a moment before deciding instead that she was exhausted. The ground welcomed her body, the earth reached up to guide her down, and for a moment she understood the calling her husband must feel. The dirt that sang in his blood. Her body had rejected it before, but now she knew how silly that was. How it belonged. How she belonged.

When Steve awoke in an empty bed the next morning his first thought was that maybe there would be breakfast, or at least coffee, ready. That was only a wish. Deep inside somewhere never to be said, because wishes like these must always remain hidden, she could have been gone forever and maybe it would be a relief. Somewhere closer to the surface he still prayed for her to be with him forever.

Nicole was not downstairs. There was no coffee, no breakfast.

"Nicole?" he asked the house.

Bewildered, he walked out the back door and onto the screened-in porch, what Nicole liked to call the sun porch. There was no one there. It was unseasonably warm. The cicadas were long gone, but the heat brought back their memory and Steve wondered if he would ever feel a hot summer morning without also hearing those very specific screams somewhere in his mind.

Outside of the sun porch they had a small patio with a grill and little else. Steve had dreams of making this a more comfortable space, but Nicole wasn't much for being in the sun. He reminded himself from time to time that everything wasn't for Nicole. And currently it seemed their entire home was not for Nicole because she was not there.

Checking the front of the house he saw her car was gone, and he felt a lump of fear and also a lump of something else. He wandered inside and made coffee, and while it was percolating, he called the local hospital and inquired if they had possibly seen his wife there. They had not. He tried to reason this meant all was well, it wasn't like Nicole never left. It wasn't until that moment he realized what he should have done immediately, which was to call her cell phone, she didn't answer. Now he was scared. The fear made him relieved. He didn't really want the other—the thing he wouldn't say out loud for fear of making a wish.

Steve sat down with his coffee. He couldn't be rational without any caffeine in his system. Nicole could be at the store or the church. Those were the two big offenders. Earlier in the year it could have been the lawn and garden store, however that wasn't as likely now. Not with the cicadas gone. He should try the church first. He'd told her to pray last night, and it was possible she was taking his advice. That would have been okay.

He finished his cup of coffee and poured another into a travel mug and made his way out to his truck. Nothing looked wrong. Everything seemed the same. He drove down to the church. It was Wednesday morning and there shouldn't be anyone there yet, not at this time.

He would have run her over if he hadn't been paying close enough attention. If he'd looked at his coffee cup or phone or admired the little church by the woods for even a moment, he would have rolled his truck directly over her chest and ankles. Steve Warby was nothing if not a cautious driver, and therefore he did see his lovely young wife laying right at the entrance to the church, her body stretched lengthwise across the gravel.

Steve stopped his truck with the back end still in the road and scrambled down into the small grey rocks to scoop up Nicole Warby's head and do nothing but hold it for a few long and painful moments. Just holding, grateful to be doing it, because who knew what the future would be—or how long it would last.

CHAPTER 5

NICOLE WARBY FELT different these days.

It was hard for her to keep track of certain things. The time of day, for example, was especially tricky. Steve had not let her leave the bed since he brought her home on Wednesday and now it was . . . definitely not Wednesday. The exact day was up for debate as far as she was concerned. Bed rest did this to people.

When Steve brought her soup, she assumed it was dinner. It could have just as easily been lunch. This did not help the matter of time. Not that it concerned her. She felt less concerned now than she had in years.

"How long have I been in this bed?"

"It's only been a couple of days."

"It feels like a month, at least."

"I promise it's only Friday."

"Oh sure, but what year?" Nicole smiled and the smile bewildered Steve. "I'm kidding, Steve. Don't worry."

"I knew that," he said, and tried to believe it.

"I honestly feel fine. And the doctor said there wasn't anything wrong with me."

"You fell asleep in a parking lot. That isn't nothing."

"I told you before, I fell asleep in the woods."

"Not better."

"Do I need to stay here forever?"

Steve didn't answer, because he didn't know the answer. He didn't know how to help his wife, who kept insisting she didn't need any help. She'd been strange recently. Now she seemed different entirely. Old nervous habits were missing, and Steve longed for them. The way she wrapped her light hair around her fingers and, when she thought no one was looking, she'd press it against her lips, not inside her mouth. He hadn't noticed her nibbling the skin around her fingernails or tapping her teeth together or checking the inside of her ears for swelling.

"You don't need to stay here forever. I don't know what to do. I want you to be well. I love you, Nicole." This was all true. Yet he left out some truth, he omitted the one thing which was most true—he did not want her to embarrass him again.

Nicole considered how often Steve told her he loved her. Every morning before he left the house, but that was a different kind of saying it. She appreciated hearing it. "I love you too," she said. She grinned. She reached for his face. "I want you to know that I'm alright." Her fingertips caressed his cheek and he smiled. He believed her. "I need to be out of this room, I'm okay. I won't scare you anymore. I'm going to be better now."

"I'd like that."

"Of course you would." And there was not accusation in her voice, only softness and mercy. "I'm going to have to leave this room. And, Steve, I don't want to worry you, but I need to go out. It's important."

"Tonight?"

"What's tomorrow? I forgot already."

"Saturday."

"I can wait until Saturday then, no worries there. We'll stay together tonight. Then tomorrow I need to run an errand. I'll keep my phone, you won't worry."

Steve was conflicted. This all sounded reasonable, and that did worry him. It shouldn't sound reasonable. But he also knew he couldn't very well keep her locked up. Nicole was going to leave. "I won't worry," he repeated. "I'd like you to not only keep your cell phone with you, but also answer it if I call. In fact, I could go with you."

"You'd only be bored. Besides, it's a surprise."

Steve nodded. Nicole closed her eyes and seemed to sink further into the bed. He watched her for a few minutes until her breathing became long and regular. The air inside the room was heavy. It sat in Steve's lungs like molasses and an alarming flash of dismay unfurled through his limbs like black smoke.

"I have to get out of here," he told the room. He took his wife's untouched bowl of soup and fled to the kitchen. His feet were lead on the stairs; the bowl of soup so heavy he was afraid he might drop it.

Once in the kitchen, he tried sitting at the old pale wooden table and retreating into nothing—but the air. He was drowning in it, hot and thick and sweet. Panic tried to rise in his chest, but it wasn't strong enough to burst through the enormous density settling into his body. Getting up slowly, fighting against the empty space, he trudged out to the sun porch.

The spell broke the moment he stepped outside, and he sucked cold air into his body and held it there, letting the oxygen absorb into his cells. He exhaled and watched the light puff of warm air float off into the night.

The porch light was off, and that was okay. The lights from the house were enough for him to see the metal patio table and chairs and he took one, sitting up normally for a few seconds, but ultimately, he laid his head down against the glass and closed his eyes. He just needed to rest—to recover.

Time passed, Steve couldn't be sure how quickly, yet he didn't let it bother him. It was his turn to be unconcerned for a moment. When he finally looked up, the lights inside the house were off. The yard was silent, as if every animal on earth was holding its breath, waiting to see what would happen. They knew something he didn't.

He rose carefully, conscious of every breath he took as he walked to the door. It was locked. At first, he simply stood there, his mind not comprehending the situation.

"Nicole?"

He thought he heard something then. A laugh from somewhere out in the dark. Or maybe it was wind chimes.

"We don't have any chimes," he told the sound.

The sound giggled and Steve tried the door handle again. Still locked.

"Screw you," Steve muttered. The air was still, but at least it wasn't thick. He could breathe, nonetheless he wasn't keen on the idea of sleeping outside.

The front door was also locked; he knew it would be. He always locked the front door the moment he stepped through it. The windows in front of the house were also locked. He had a garage door opener in his truck, unfortunately the truck was locked and his keys were inside the house. He sighed in frustration, trying to decide which door or window would be best to break into—what would be the least expensive to replace. He rapped loudly on the front door without much hope.

"Nicole!" he yelled. The house remained dark. "Hey, Nicole!"

Nothing.

He listened again for the wind chimes, holding his breath. And there it was.

Something.

A tinkle of something light and playful. It was coming from the fields, and without any reason or thought, he went to it. He could see every star in the galaxy ahead of him as he plodded south toward the nearest cornfield. The stalks were tall dry ghosts waiting to be exorcised. They would have flitted in the wind if there had been any. Steve hesitated for only a second before stepping into the rows, following the only sound left in the world.

The stalks reached out and caressed his cheeks. The dirt below him was loose and soft. He took slow, even paces because he was afraid he'd trip over something in the dark. He looked up at the stars, but they had dimmed. He could only see three or four now, and the path ahead of him was getting darker by the second.

He could make out something in front of him, a thin silhouette standing between the rows about twenty yards ahead. It hadn't been there and then it was. It popped into existence and tried to convince Steve it had always been in the field—he knew better. He wasn't going to be tricked by any shadows.

"Nicole?" His question was a whisper—he didn't want an answer. Whatever was here, he didn't want to know it. He took a step backward, then he heard it—the laughter, the chimes.

The shadow in front of him slowly swayed back and forth. The feet firmly planted, the body leaning impossibly far to the left, then right, then back. Slow, slow—how did it not fall?

Steve was too afraid to look away. He took long deliberate steps backward. When he thought he'd gone far enough to chance a look around, he saw he must still be deep in the field. The house was nowhere. He stretched up on his tiptoes and looked over the field, still all he could see was dark. A yelp escaped him when he looked back at the shape. It was closer now, so close he might have touched it if he reached. But he didn't. It was still solid black, no features or shapes or shadows. Just darkness in a way Steve had never seen before. Darkness like he could walk right into it.

His breath came out in hard hot bursts. He gaped at the thing in front of him and began his retreat once again. Stepping backward, trying to keep himself under control, trying not to break and run or fall or die. It kept receding from him, but he still wasn't out of the corn and that seemed impossible. He stopped. He lifted himself onto his toes. He looked behind him.

There was no house.

No light.

No sky.

Only darkness and corn and the shape swaying gently from side to side—now only three feet in front of him.

"Go away," Steve whispered.

The shape stopped swaying and stood tall. Laughter like wind chimes filled the air and Steve could no longer stay calm. He turned and ran toward where the house ought to be, his vision locked on the ground in front of him, his legs pumping until the dirt changed to grass and he looked up so suddenly he lost his balance and fell, tumbling over and over himself—limbs and spit flying. There it was, larger than life and *real.* His old two-story farmhouse loomed from the darkness and every light was on. He pulled himself from the ground and ran to the open front door. Nicole was there holding it open wide for him.

"Hello, lover," she purred as he exploded inside.

Nicole closed the door behind him and leaned back against it.

"You locked me out," he gasped.

"Why would I do that?"

"What?" Blood was ringing in his ears.

"Come to bed, darling. You aren't well."

Steve allowed his wife to lead him up the steps to the bedroom. In the hallway she stepped behind him and gently nudged him toward the door. A soft whisper in his ear, "This is not real."

"Is everything okay?" Nicole asked, sitting up in the bed.

Steve whipped his head back and gazed, stunned, at an empty hallway.

"This is not really happening," he said.

"You bet your life it is," Nicole replied.

"I think I was having a dream." He rubbed his eyes with the heel of his palms. As his vision blurred then refocused on his wife laying in the bed right where he'd left her earlier in the evening, everything else seemed to come into focus as well. "I guess I fell asleep on the porch and had a nightmare." He offered a sheepish smile.

"Things are really starting now," Nicole said, and laid her head back on the pillow.

Steve walked to the bedroom window and looked out toward the fields to the south. It was time to harvest that field, first thing in the morning. Nicole had her mystery errands to run, and he had a field to tend. He squinted and imagined a shape tik-toking at the edge of the lawn. Just his imagination.

On Saturdays, Sara Douglas did the grocery shopping. She planned out her family's meals for each day and made a list ordering the items as they appeared in the store. A couple of years ago the Walmart had rearranged the grocery section and it ruined her entire month.

Lilin didn't have any grocery stores outside of Walmart and the small market inside the Dollar General. Sara had to be sure that whatever recipes she was using that week didn't contain any specialty items she couldn't get at one of the two places. Not that they usually did. The stores always stocked potatoes and beans—and she could do a lot with those.

After the store, Sara would work on the lesson plan for the women's group and deep-clean the kitchen and bathrooms. That was the routine and it suited her. Her life had become comfortable once she'd accepted those routines. Her husband, Paul, would be out all day Saturday with church council business. Back when the twins were little, this bothered her. She'd complain to him about needing help, a day off. Yet he taught her something back then she would never forget. That doing it yourself made you strong.

One day, in a fit of doubt and tears, she had screamed at him, "Where do you think you're going? What's so important?"

And Paul had smiled at her and placed a hand on her shoulder. He cupped her cheek in his callused hand and said, "Sara, God has called me for this work. And he has called you to be my wife. Are you going to turn your back on your work?"

She'd broken down sobbing and Paul had left her there. He'd left her in a pile on the floor with two one-year-old boys. When her tears dried up and her husband was still gone, she did the work that she had to do—because there was no other choice. And eventually she discovered she was good at the work. She built her routines and her schedules and, in time, it became her everything. She was strong because she had to be, and because God had called her to be Paul Douglas' wife. She didn't question His will anymore.

It was busier than usual at the store. There was no good reason for it—no storms in the forecast, not the first of the month—and it annoyed Sara. She wheeled her cart back to the lawn and garden section because she needed new gardening gloves and was surprised to see Nicole Warby wandering through the aisles with no shopping cart. Her attention was focused on a display of outdoor decorations—gnomes and flags and ceramic toadstools—and she was wearing jeans and a faded Bon Jovi t-shirt with a hole in the left side.

"Nicole, are you feeling okay?"

"Why, what have you heard?"

Sara stared.

"Sorry, yes, I feel fine. I was a little under the weather maybe before, but I'm fine now."

"Well, that's good to hear. We missed y'all on Wednesday." Sara put a very specific smile in place and held it.

"Oh yeah, we missed you all too. I'm better. I'll be there on Tuesday, don't you worry."

"I never do," Sara said, and believed it. "Okay, I'll let you get back to it. I've got a million things to tend to."

"Absolutely, good to see you."

Sara watched as Nicole continued wandering through the aisles with no clear agenda. It was sad, honestly. The poor thing needed direction. Lord knew she'd tried. She'd tried to prepare her for kids, to give her responsibility in the women's group, to guide her. Although Nicole seemed to have her own ideas.

That was fine. Sara didn't have time to worry about Nicole Warby or her apparent inability to be a proper wife. She had bigger things to worry about. Her husband would be gone all day, and while she no longer wanted his help at home, she still feared for the day his Saturday activities would impact her family. She trusted God to keep them safe. God trusted her to make dinner.

Nicole returned home Saturday evening with bags full of clanging metal.

"What is all this?" Steve asked.

"It's wind chimes."

"For the patio?" Steve's stomach clenched. The chimes gave him a sense of dread he couldn't quite place. He felt the floor shift then he remembered—his dream. Something sinister to do with wind chimes. But that didn't seem right. What could be sinister about those?

"For anything."

She had five different chimes and she placed one on the front porch, one on the back porch, and the other three from low hanging branches in the back yard.

"I don't understand why you had to make a special trip for a bag full of wind chimes." Steve was sulking though he knew it wasn't reasonable. Something in his heart told him to hate those chimes.

"I needed them," was all Nicole would say.

"Why does anyone need a wind chime?"

"The same reason we need anything. We just do. Sometimes you need things."

He wasn't getting anywhere and decided to accept the new decorations. His wife was in a good mood and it's not like the purchases were bothering him, at least not in any way he would allow himself to understand. It seemed odd. Not sleeping in a parking lot or eating dirt odd, but odd nonetheless.

"I think maybe you should see that therapist the doctor recommended," Steve said, hoping he sounded casual.

"We can't afford that."

"We should make it a priority. I can move some stuff around; we can make it work."

"You know therapy isn't a one and done sort of situation. I'd have to go a bunch. Let's not think about it anymore. I don't think it's important. I was probably in a mood before."

"A dirt-eating mood?" He didn't want it to sound mean, yet he knew it did. And maybe he did want it to.

"I told you before I didn't eat dirt." Her voice rose slightly, and Steve was happy to hear anything other than passive mild tones coming from his wife.

"Then how'd it get inside you? The same way you got in the parking lot?"

"I'm going to go make dinner. And you're going to forget about this."

Nicole left the room without another word, and he was left there feeling nervous for no reason at all. But there had been a reason, though not one he could talk about. The only friends he had in Lilin were members of the church, and he wasn't sure they considered him a friend. His only desires in this life were to work in the dirt and be part of a community. The community he had chosen was the Lilin Assembly of Our Lord and taking part in it meant not making waves. Paul told the same jokes every Wednesday. Church events were held on the same days at the same times.

In Lilin, you did not talk to your friends about ghosts in the cornfield. You didn't tell them you were afraid or that you thought maybe the ghosts were getting into the house at night along with the occasional field mice. No, that was the sort of business you kept to yourself. Because saying it out loud made it real and, oh God, he did not want it to be real. There was only one accepted supernatural being to be discussed and that was God Himself—and maybe the occasional witch.

As Nicole cooked dinner she listened intently for the new chimes in her yard. So many of them together made a light dissonant symphony that soothed her. She wished she could explain to Steve why she needed them, but knew he would never understand. Things were changing for her—they had already changed. She didn't feel like the same soft, directionless child who had moved to Lilin. It had started in the woods.

When she'd seen those shoes she wasn't supposed to see. The same shoes that wouldn't be there again if she went looking, because they didn't belong there. Not in that place, not in that time. Those shoes were a whisper.

She understood things about the woods now. Once she'd been afraid of them, thought they were evil. Woods are not good or evil—they simply are. They take in what they are given and sometimes they absorb or even reflect. They do not create. That is left to man. Man trusts his creation is always a gift out of arrogance, believing all they conjure is good simply because it comes from them. Sometimes they create the very monsters they fear. Even the wickedest man believes he is good—creating justification after justification for every sin under the moon. And the woods are simply there to observe and keep and hold.

Nicole was now a thing to be held by those woods. And it was better by far than being held by the men who met there.

After dinner Steve fell asleep on the couch and dreamed again (for the first time) about the chimes. The whole world was hollow tones, glittering in the sunshine and something different in the moonlight. In the moonlight they slid. In the trees and through the air, they slipped into places they hadn't been before and built nests.

When he awoke, it was past midnight. The air in the house felt stagnant and he was sweating. A light was on in the kitchen and as he moved to turn it off something out in the yard caught his eye. Nicole was in the tree.

"What the fuck is going on?" he mumbled.

His wife was hunched on one of the low thick limbs of the gum tree just to the left of the patio. He was seeing her through the glass of the kitchen and the screens of the sun porch, but it was her, knees up around her ears, hands holding onto her ankles. He couldn't tell if she was wearing anything at all—her edges bled together. She peered at him, and he thought she must be glowing—because exactly how *could* he see her in the dark? The kitchen light illuminated some of the yard, though not into the trees. Even if the moon was completely full, and he didn't think it was, he shouldn't be able to see her so plainly.

Fear, irrational and hard, gripped his heart. He had to go get his wife out of the tree, but he didn't want to. As ashamed as he felt, he couldn't deny that what he really wanted to do was lock the door and turn off the lights. Let her stay there and be weird all on her own. She could leave him out of whatever this was.

"Penny for your thoughts?"

Steve screamed and leapt away from the voice.

"Wow, you're jumpy." Nicole stood directly behind him, her gaze far away, a tiny smile playing across her lips. She slid to the refrigerator, and retrieved a small bottle of cranberry juice.

Steve didn't respond, just looked back through the window. He didn't see anything in the trees except for the wind chimes. Fear filled his chest again, although this time it was different. This time it was worse. It was the kind of fear that slips into your heart when you're confused and alone. The shortness of breath you feel when you don't know what to do and the situation is hopeless.

"I gotta check the yard," he said.

He didn't turn on any lights, deciding that his eyesight would be more reliable once it adjusted to the night. The tree was annoyingly average. Steve didn't know what he hoped to find, but it sure wasn't nothing.

Nicole was next to him now. She had on solid white cotton pajamas that buttoned up the front. She sipped her juice loudly and Steve had to stop himself from telling her not to spill like he would a child.

"What's out here?" she asked.

"I don't guess I know. I sure thought I saw something, though. I sure did . . ." His voice trailed away, and he looked instead up into the sky hoping to see a bird or a dinosaur or anything at all to make things feel okay again.

"Sometimes I think I see things too," Nicole whispered.

He looked back at her and for a moment he thought there was juice all over her top. And in another moment it was blood. And in another moment it was clean as fresh snow.

"I think I should get some sleep."

"Why don't I make the breakfast in the morning?" Nicole suggested. Her lips were a little too red. Or at least Steve thought they were.

"That'd be nice, but don't put yourself out. We'll see whoever gets up first. No pressure." He said all this as he walked back into the house, and it wasn't until he'd finished the last sentence that he realized his wife was not behind him listening. He turned around and there she was, not in the tree now, huddled under it, hugging herself in a tight little ball. His first thought was about how dirty her pajamas would get, and the absurdity made him laugh and the laughter made him nervous. He was cracking up.

"Nicole?" he called to her.

She raised one of her arms and waved at him, long and

dramatic like she was on a desert island and flagging down a rescue ship.

"Penny for your thoughts," he whispered. He closed the door and walked deeper into the house. The only things on the second floor were the master bed and bathrooms. He decided that it was time to go to bed.

Nicole stood on the staircase landing. She was pushed back into the corner, up on her tiptoes. The sound of her teeth chattering sounded like broken morse code. The flash of her jaw as she chopped faster and faster was impossible. "You're going to hurt your feet doing that," he said, but he meant to say teeth. Too late now.

And from the kitchen, Nicole said, "Who needs feet, anyway?"

In the bedroom it looked like Nicole was under the blankets already. He could hear her soft deep breathing, except the longer he listened the more it sounded like growling.

"Listen, I'll stay on my side and you stay on yours," he told the room. He slipped under the covers and closed his eyes tight.

"You know, honey," Nicole whispered in his ear, "I don't think there are any witches in the woods. None at all."

Bright light was in his eyes and Steve opened one wearily. It seemed like the sun. Though he already knew his vision wasn't trustworthy. On the other hand, his sense of smell hadn't failed him yet, and it told him there was coffee in the house.

It was full daylight. The room was practically on fire. The clock told him it was already 9am. In all this brightness, all the oddness of the night before seemed like a dream that was fading fast from his memory. It was a dream. He'd fallen asleep on the couch and had a nightmare. These things happened. A little too often these days.

Downstairs, Nicole was sitting at the table with a cup

of coffee and the newspaper. There was a box of donuts and a pitcher of orange juice on the counter.

"Did you go out?" he asked.

"Well, they certainly didn't deliver the donuts. Or the paper for that matter. Don't we normally get a Sunday paper?"

"We don't get a paper at all, we don't subscribe."

"Good thing I picked one up then. Look, I know I said I'd cook breakfast. I know I did and I'm the absolute worst. But I didn't feel like it today. And it occurred to me I couldn't think of anything nicer than coffee and donuts and the Sunday paper. That felt like the sweetest idea in the whole world this morning. So that's what I did. I hope you don't mind."

Steve smiled and poured a cup of coffee. "I like donuts every now and then. Do you mind if I take a section you aren't looking at?"

"Not at all!"

"We've got some time before we need to get to church, do you want to sit on the porch with this?"

"Sure," she answered. "Why don't we skip church today? It's really pretty out. We could relax a little on the porch, take our time with breakfast."

"Yeah, but the porch will still be here after services. Maybe we'll pick up something from the deli on the way home. We could have a picnic."

"I don't want to go to the church." A second ago she'd practically been purring, now the claws were out.

He didn't know how fried his nerves were until he snapped at her. "You were happy enough to sleep there a few days ago!"

"Shut up, Steve."

"Excuse me? Since when do we talk to each other like this? What's gotten into you?"

"Absolutely nothing. I don't feel like going to that stupid church for one stupid day. It's all we ever do."

"That's not my fault. You can do other stuff."

“Are you kidding me? You made us move out here away from everything. Away from my friends and family.”

Steve laughed and it sounded like loathing. “What family? You haven’t talked to your mom in years.”

“And now I can’t talk to anyone, so I hope you’re happy.”

“You told me you wanted to move out here.”

“What else was I supposed to say? Would you have stayed if I asked?” She knew the answer before she asked, but she didn’t know if Steve did.

He thought for a few long seconds. “No, I wouldn’t have.”

“Would you have divorced me?”

“No, you were going to come with me.” He said all this like he was reading lines from a script for the first time. It was all news to Steve. “You didn’t have a reason to stay, and besides, I’m in charge, right?”

“And I’m just the submissive wife, huh?”

“Let’s go to church.” He didn’t want her to answer. He plodded back upstairs to get dressed. Why was this happening? Why were they fighting? The world didn’t feel entirely real anymore.

He took a shower and when he got out Nicole was sitting on the bed and dressed in a long black skirt, a short-sleeved white blouse, and a pale pink cardigan. She was looking at her hands, trying to figure out what they were.

“I’m sorry,” she said.

“I’m sorry too. I didn’t mean what I said.”

“Which part?”

“Any of it. We don’t have to go to church today if you don’t want to. I’m not sure why I’m being this way. Maybe I’m not feeling myself either.”

“Maybe you’re more yourself than ever. I’m ready for church now, so we may as well go. You’re right, the porch will be here when we get back. I’m sure nothing will be different.”

Of course nothing would be different, it went without saying. Nothing was ever very different in Lilin.

This Sunday felt alarmingly like the last one, and Steve understood all at once, sitting there in their usual pew, looking out the windows at the same view as ever, why it was Nicole might not feel like being back quite so soon. He felt like a jackass.

The organ music began, and the procession made its way to the front of the sanctuary. The choir had new robes this week. They looked the same as the old ones, only a little fresher.

Today they started things off by singing "What a Friend We Have in Jesus." Nicole was happy because she knew all the words without even looking at the hymnal. People often say it is the little things that make life worth living. Nicole did not generally believe this was true. The things that made her the happiest could usually be traced back to big things. Movie night on the couch might sound like a small thing, but they had to purchase the house, couch, and television before any of it was possible, and none of these were small things. Big things enabled small things to be nice.

Reverend Grey stood before his congregation and quietly took them all in, as if deciding if they were worthy of today's message.

"Today, we shall consider First Peter, chapter three: 'Wives, in the same way submit yourselves to your own husbands so that, if any of them do not believe the word, they may be won over without words by the behavior of their wives, when they see the purity and reverence of your lives.' Here we are instructed on what wives should do if their husbands become disobedient to the Lord. If your husbands do not believe the word, here is your manual on how to save them! Isn't that glorious?"

A few members of the congregation nodded, no one spoke.

"What is it a wife should do? First, she should make sure that her own behavior is pure and reverent. If we read a little further, Peter tells us she should be 'gentle and quiet.'" His gaze seemed to land on Nicole, and she looked back at him thinking only gentle thoughts.

"We should read further, and feel free to follow along in your own Bibles. I'm going to continue in Peter, chapter three. 'Husbands, in the same way be considerate as you live with your wives, and treat them with respect as the weaker partner and as heirs with you of the gracious gift of life, so that nothing will hinder your prayers.' You see? He still instructs husbands to respect women for what they are. You must be considerate of your wives.

"And now here is our final thought from Peter for today. 'Finally, all of you, be like-minded, be sympathetic, love one another, be compassionate and humble. Do not repay evil with evil or insult with insult. On the contrary, repay evil with blessing, because to this you were called so that you may inherit a blessing.'

"What are we instructing our wives to do? Let's break these parts down, because I believe they are so important. Firstly, she should never retaliate against her husband. If he is cross with her, she shouldn't be cross in return or try to punish him with silence or passive aggressive fake kindness. No, a wife should always be a blessing to her husband. If she is angry and bitter, then she is not doing God's will. God himself has instructed our wives to be quiet and not to argue. To submit and be only a blessing.

"But as I said, there are instructions for husbands too. A wife should never join her husband in sinful behavior. If your husband is sinning, you may be a quiet and Godly example to him. If your husband is yelling at you, then you must be certain you are not provoking him with your words or behavior—unless it is by your sweet and Godly behavior. In Peter it says to win your husbands over without a word. Meaning not to nag him, not to argue and fight. Instead bring him, through your submission and goodness, back to a life of faith."

Steve's mind was wandering. That morning his wife hadn't exactly been quiet, and it was true that his yelling hadn't made anything any better. If she had just been quiet, he wondered if maybe he would have been able to get on the right track. It felt silly to think about, but Reverend Grey did tell them to be like-minded. If this was what his friends in the church believed, maybe it was right. His resistance might very well be the Devil trying to trick him. He smiled at the last thought. That sounded like the right thing to say, still it felt silly. He looked at Nicole and smiled. She smiled at him and then turned her attention back to the reverend. There didn't seem to be any nausea today and that felt like a good sign.

After the service, members of the church took time to shake hands and greet each other before heading out to the parking lot, where more greetings and conversations took place. After sitting in mostly silence for an hour, it felt nice to smile at people and make small talk.

"Heck of a sermon today, wasn't it?" Andrew Cole said to Steve, shaking his hand.

"It sure was a lot to think on," Steve agreed.

"It makes sense, doesn't it? I'm sitting there thinking about how every time Charity asks me to mow the lawn, well, it's the absolute last thing I want to do. But if I mow it and she talks about how nice it looks or whatever then I feel like I want to do it."

"Is that what this was about? That's, uh . . . there's a name for it." Steve frowned at the floor for a few seconds before his face lit up. "Positive reinforcement!"

"Maybe." Andrew shrugged.

"Sometimes I feel like Reverend should say what he means. Because I was getting a little confused toward the end. If this is all some basic marriage counseling stuff, I think I get it."

"Is that right?" Paul asked. He walked up behind Steve and clapped him on the back.

"Yeah, absolutely. It's not about submitting; it's about feeling appreciated. Instead of feeling obligated, feeling like you want to do something. Like if your wife makes you think it was your idea to go out to dinner or whatever."

"I don't know if that was it." Andrew was frowning.

"Things are always up for a little interpretation," Paul said. "Just a little," and he winked. "I'll tell you what's not, though, this beautiful day we've been given. Let's get out of this stuffy building."

Andrew watched the two men walk out the big double doors and felt something hard inside his chest. Who was this Warby guy? He was some big city rich kid come out here to slum it and pretend to be a farmer until he got bored or spent all his daddy's money. Who was he to tell him what a sermon meant? A sermon from a church he'd attended his whole life. His parents had gone to this church until his mother went to be with Jesus and his father went to be with the Silver Birch nursing home. The farm he tended had belonged to his grandfather. Lilin was his home.

He looked over at his wife and felt the hardness melt a little. She was beautiful and he loved her. He'd never given much thought to submission in their marriage, that was because she'd always been a good wife. She didn't run around puking in the sanctuary like Steve's wife. What a mess that woman was. If anyone needed to be shown how a wife should behave, it was Nicole Warby.

Outside the church, Nicole Warby had gravitated toward her husband and was lingering by his side as he spoke to Paul about harvesting, or soil samples, or market prices, or something else she didn't care or know about.

"Nicole, I wanted to say that Sara and I have been keeping you in our prayers this week. I hope you've been feeling better," Paul said.

"Thank you so much, I have been. Just a little bit of a bug, I think."

"Absolutely. And on another note, I hope you didn't feel too put out about the way things went the other day."

"What things?" she asked.

"Well, about the council. I'm sure you understand, that's not the place for a woman." Paul grinned and patted her shoulder and Nicole felt a hot wave of revulsion sweep over her.

"Water under the bridge," Steve said.

Nicole didn't say anything in reply. Instead, her thoughts were drawn to the wind. There had been a shift and she smelled something new coming in. The soft constant sound of the woods—insects and birds and squirrels and the rustle of leaves both living and dead—faded until there was no sound at all. Something new was coming in.

Nicole turned her attention toward the back of the lot, toward the woods, and she saw other people seemed to be doing the same thing. The primal part of the brain, the part that still reacted on instinct and warned of danger approaching, had signaled to be on the lookout. As Nicole gazed into the green on brown collage before her, something different emerged, something new. She couldn't identify it at first. It was just color moving behind the leaves, soft rosy cream gliding closer, becoming larger as it approached. Nicole took a step forward, but Steve snatched her hand, holding her in place.

It wasn't until Sara Douglas screamed that the image started to come together for Nicole. It was a woman. A nude woman. She'd reached the edge of the parking lot now and Nicole winced as her bare feet hit the gravel, although the woman did not seem to notice. She had long blonde hair that stood up at odd angles because the tangles had gotten so big. The bones of her body jutted at sharp angles, every rib on perfect display, every tendon and vein popping out of the thin layer of flesh desperately trying to keep it contained. Dirt was caked on her legs and stomach. The woman stumbled forward on legs that didn't look sturdy enough to support her. Her right hand was covering her crotch and Nicole thought it odd to be modest about that when her tiny breasts were on full display as well.

"Steve, she's sick," Nicole said, and pulled her hand away from his. He seemed too stunned to react or stop her.

Nicole took slow, deliberate steps toward the woman. "Are you okay? Can we help you?"

The woman stopped then. Nicole took her cardigan off and held it out to the woman, an offering and a shield.

The hand that had been at her crotch raised then. The fingers were smeared with thick dark red blood.

"She's hurt," someone yelled. "Call an ambulance!"

She held her bloody fingers up next to her face and tears started to trail from her eyes making slow paths through the dirt on her cheeks. "God is good," the woman whispered.

Nicole summoned her courage and took a few more bold steps until she was standing next to the woman. "Here, put this on." She draped the cardigan over her shoulders.

The woman's eyes widened and she screamed, "God is good! God is good! God is good!" Her words became stilted with sobs.

Nicole leapt backward.

The hand had gone back between her legs, and she raised it with even more blood. Falling to her knees, her sobs turned to something more like laughter without joy—hard and mean. She put her fingers to her lips and slowly wiped the blood into her mouth. "Hallelujah," she cried. "I am free. God is good, hallelujah."

Nicole hesitated then knelt next to the woman. The rocks cut into her knees. "You're going to be okay," Nicole said.

Steve was standing next to his wife now. "Honey, don't get too close."

"Why?"

"She could be . . . " What? Dangerous? Diseased? Hexed? All of these seemed probable.

"Stay back from her." This was Reverend Grey. "A woman like this coming from those cursed woods is nothing to take lightly."

Charity hurried toward Nicole and huddled next to her.

"Let's go, dear. Someone is on the way. Let the men handle this."

"I don't think the men should be the ones caring for this poor soul," Nicole said.

The nude woman on the ground was listening to them. Her eyes flashed from one speaker to the next. "There is a house in the woods," she told them.

"What? Where?" Nicole asked.

"There is a house in the woods, covered in moss and time. It is a cursed place, and it hurries. There is a house in the woods where not even crickets will chirp. It is hurrying."

"The witches," Reverend Grey said.

"No," the woman said, so low it was a moan. "It will catch you." Nicole marveled at the words coming from this emaciated and delirious person. Her gums and teeth were stained with blood, and just as she thought to offer her some water, the woman fainted. She would have thought she was dead, except her body was so frail the ragged rise and fall of her lungs was horrifyingly distinct.

"We should really get a doctor or a nurse as a member," Donna said, and it was so practical it sounded obscene.

Nicole looked out into the woods. She was remembering the shoes she'd seen the other night. But also something else, something out of place. It was right on the edges of her mind, only it refused to come into focus. The peculiar feeling of starting a puzzle with the center instead of the edges rose inside her. "Things aren't right."

"Reverend Grey, do you know what's out in those woods?" Andrew asked. "An old house, right? Maybe the police should be searching it."

"How would I know?" was all the reverend said.

"I'm sure they'll check it out," Paul said. "In the meantime, we really need to stay inside. There could be someone dangerous out there."

"I'd say she's the dangerous one," said Sara, and Nicole couldn't shake the idea she was talking about her.

Nicole needed to get back into the woods, only she didn't know how to get there. Somewhere inside there was a house. There were (shoes) creatures. There was something keenly alive. And it was hurrying.

"I don't think I've ever seen anything like that," Steve said.

He and Nicole had been sitting at their kitchen table in silence for hours. She didn't say so, but Nicole thought maybe she had seen something similar. The sky was an inky grey-blue and the leaves had turned themselves over, heralding the storm rolling in across the fields. The edges were softer in the rain.

"Are the police searching the woods?"

"Paul told me they were going to be out there looking, I imagine this weather is going to slow them down though. If there was someone out there, they're probably long gone by now."

"A whole house doesn't disappear," she said—not adding, only thinking, *even if it does move around.*

"The Coles did say something about a fort being out there, didn't they?"

"I don't think they said 'fort.' But something. A stone building."

"Could be squatters holed up inside."

"That sounds reasonable."

"Maybe your women's group could do something for that lady. Send flowers?" The suggestion felt lame.

"We could visit. It might be nice for her to have some female company."

"The way she was bleeding . . . I just . . . I've never seen anything . . . "

"It was menstrual," Nicole said without knowing she was going to say it.

"How do you know that?"

"I don't. And I do. It feels right."

Steve shuddered.

The chimes in the trees were giving a performance as the wind picked up and swirled them into a frenzy. It seemed like there were more of them than there had been before. In fact, Steve was positive the one with the blue glass on the front porch hadn't been there when they left earlier that day, yet he was afraid to mention it. Sometimes you didn't want to be right.

Steve reached across the table and held his wife's hand. It was so small, yet it felt like so much. The heat of her skin helped him know his was also hot. Feeling her live reminded him to keep living. Sometimes he needed the reminder, sometimes he was afraid he might fade away without it. She squeezed his hand and smiled at him even though it was the last thing she wanted to do. The weight of his hand, and the need within that hand, was almost too much. It could have crushed her.

"There are things in Lilin I never expected," she said.

"Lilin didn't ask for them."

"No one ever asks anymore."

The rain had started.

"Jesus. I need a drink." Steve stood up, plodded to the fridge and pulled out a beer.

"It's three o'clock on a Sunday," Nicole said. It was not an accusation so much as a realization.

"I had a dream last night," Steve said. "I don't remember all of it, much at all, only I can't help but feel it was something about today."

The air inside the house was trying to talk. It was thrumming in their ears, making them dizzy. If the pressure would change, ease to a ringing instead of that full rippling *wom-wom-wom,* it would be better. Steve felt nauseous, too hot, unsteady.

"I'm afraid I might throw up," Nicole said.

Steve nodded. It was like being car sick. Nothing in the stomach, everything in the inner ear. It still ended the same.

"I have to get out of this house," she said. She stood up so abruptly her chair clattered to the floor, and she didn't bother with picking it up. She ran out into the back yard and fell onto the grass, retching. Wind whipped her hair into her mouth, and she clawed it back out as quickly as possible. She looked up at the sky. The clouds were a wall, despite that she could see definition in between them enough to notice how quickly they were moving. Things were going to happen fast.

"Are you okay?" Steve asked from the doorway.

Nicole scrambled to her feet. "Yes, I feel better. I don't know what that was about."

"I felt it too."

"Maybe we should go for a walk. Fresh air."

"It's about to storm."

Nicole looked back at the sky. Tears burned the corners of her eyes. "I want to go to the woods," she said.

"Are you nuts?" He wanted it to sound harsh. Even harsher than it had.

Nicole walked past him into the house. "I'm perfectly fine," she said as she settled back at the table. "I felt a little too warm. We should really put the air on."

"It'll cool off once it starts raining."

"It's humid though."

"That'll taper off too." Steve decided the pressure in his ears was from the impending rain. Of course it was. Things made sense.

"I think I'll go up and take a nap."

"Good idea."

Nicole climbed the stairs slowly, trying to think of a way to escape the house without her husband noticing. She made it to her bedroom without a plan and suddenly did feel very tired. She stripped off her clothes and folded herself into the blankets nude. The crisp sheets felt smooth and cool against her skin. Eyes closed, legs leisurely swishing, Nicole slipped peacefully into a dream.

There was a small stone house in the woods. Not a fort

at all, a house made to withstand time and elements. Bright green moss climbed its walls and inched close to the windowpanes, and maybe eventually it would get inside. But not now. Now it was sunny, and the trees were not too thick. There were no moss-covered shoes yet. The stone house was full of life. And the lives inside the house were full.

A woman lived inside the house, and her name was not important. How she looked or what she weighed didn't matter—not then and certainly not now. She was happy there in the stone house. The average person might say she was alone, except that was not right. She had guests. Women from Lilin would come calling when they had a problem, and the lady of the stone house was usually obliged to help.

The inside of the house smelled rich, like burnt herbs and thick stew. Nicole stood in the center of the warm stone house and breathed deep. There was something else in the air, something more threatening.

"Stupid men," Nicole thought. "You can't burn a stone house."

But you can burn a woman.

Nicole jumped from the bed in a frenzy, screaming.

Downstairs, Steve heard her and decided to stay where he was. Sometimes things needed to sort themselves out. In a few hours he could go to sleep then wake up and go to work. Once he could get back out to the fields everything was going to be okay. Things could sort themselves right out.

Eventually his wife would stop screaming.

CHAPTER 6

THE WOMEN MET at Sara's house on Tuesday because they didn't know what else to do. The room was the same as ever, except the air felt thin and so did the nerves. Nicole took notice of a scented candle on the mantle, yet whatever scent was meant to lazily waft through the space was drowned out by the metallic tang of fear.

"Did the police find anything in the woods?" Charity asked.

"I haven't heard," Sara said.

"I thought Paul probably would have told you if they did."

"Paul isn't a police officer."

"I know that. But he's who called them, right?"

"I imagine that if they were going to report anything to anyone it would be Reverend Grey."

"Wouldn't he tell Paul?"

"Oh my God, Charity, I have no idea!" Sara snapped. Her jaw moved quickly as she worked to regain control. "I'm sorry. It's been a stressful week."

"It's only Tuesday," Donna said.

Sara sighed and turned her eyes to the wall in front of her. Her lips were pursed, and Nicole thought she was holding back tears. "It's felt like much longer," she said, trying to be kind. I don't mind saying, seeing that woman out there like that has me a little, well, I feel a little—" Sara's voice cracked as a tear broke free and rolled down her cheek.

"Me too," Charity said, and reached out to pat her friend's hand. She'd known Sara Douglas since she was Sara Jones, and while she wasn't always the easiest person to love, time filled in those holes that kindness left empty.

"I don't want to sound spooky, but all the witch talk is starting to feel a lot less metaphorical."

"Donna, don't be morbid," Sara said.

"I'm not. Seeing her come out of the woods like that . . . it feels a lot more likely there's some kind of coven out there."

"I don't even know what a coven is." A tiny nervous laugh bubbled out of Charity.

"We're a coven," Nicole said.

"Shut up," Sara snapped.

Donna's eyes cut over to Charity, Charity refused to meet them.

"A coven," Nicole stated, "is just a group of women that have meetings."

"A group of witches," Sara corrected.

"Think about it, we pass down recipes and counsel from the old mothers and look forward to passing on those legacies. All this submissive wife stuff is pretty close to witchcraft without the fun, if you ask me. Homemaking, healing, providing wisdom and guidance—I think those things probably apply to both equally."

"Not the submissive part," Donna said. "I don't imagine witches submit."

"That's true," Nicole said. "I guess they have one up on us there."

"Don't talk that way," Sara interjected.

"Steve and I were thinking maybe the women's group should go visit her in the hospital. It'd be very Christian of us."

The other three women in the room went silent. Nicole scanned the ground for bugs. She was determined not to be the first to speak. She didn't need to justify her suggestion. Let them squirm. They didn't deserve her salvation. Someone would eventually have to say something.

"We don't know her," Charity finally mumbled.

"Jesus didn't know basically any of the people he helped."

"I'm not Jesus, Nicole. Not by a long shot," Donna said.

"We're none of us Jesus," Sara said. "That shouldn't stop us from trying. Nicole's right. It's the Christian thing to do. We'll go tomorrow evening."

"Tomorrow is fellowship," Charity whined.

"And I'm sure we'll be done in time for dinner, we only need to drop off some flowers and magazines. For all we know she's still out of her mind."

"Nicole, didn't you say you heard voices in those woods?" It was Charity, suddenly perked up, a potluck dinner the furthest thing from her mind.

"I thought I did."

"Well, maybe it was this woman, or whoever hurt her?"

"It sounded like a woman calling my name."

"Gives me chills," Charity said, shaking her head.

"It was my imagination. More silly thoughts in a silly head. There's nothing in those woods except squirrels."

Donna stood up. "Sara, do you keep any wine in this house? I think it's about time we voted to make these meetings wet."

"It's Tuesday, Donna," Sara said. But then she, too, got to her feet and trekked into the kitchen and pulled a bottle of cheap chardonnay out of a high cabinet. The cap twisted off, no corks here, no sir, we are not putting on any airs here in Lilin. Sara brought the bottle out and handed it to Donna. "Are you fine drinking from the bottle?"

"Of course, just like middle school," and she dropped Sara a wink. Donna took a swig and handed the bottle to Charity. "I think we've all earned it this week."

"Don't tell Andrew, he's weird about me drinking."

"*He's* weird," Sara laughed, and the laugh scared her, and she clapped a hand over her mouth. "Oh, Charity, I didn't mean that. I'm sorry. Hand me that bottle."

Nicole smiled. It was the lightest and heaviest she'd ever seen these women. They were more themselves tonight. The shock and fear and worry tore down their shields and made them smaller and bigger all at once. Nicole could see the young girls they must have been not so long ago. All those dreams still held tight in their chests. When the bottle reached her, she took a drink despite hating white wine. They were sharing something tonight. An invisible ribbon was slowly weaving itself around them, tying them together, pulling them tight. This was magic, this is what true spell work meant. Not chants and blood sacrifices—a ritual between friends.

"Okay, fine," Donna said. "Tomorrow we'll go see the crazy woman from the woods. We'll bring her flowers and chocolates and when we find out where she lives, we'll take turns bringing casseroles. That's what our coven does, right?" The last part was supposed to be light, though it wasn't.

The ladies left Sara's house a little different than they'd arrived.

Nicole drove out to the church parking lot. She could go now without Steve worrying. Although she wasn't sure he'd even be worried anymore. He was tired of being worried. Concern takes an awful lot of energy. Tonight would be a good chance for him to recharge his battery while she was away.

The bright glowing cross radiated out from the church and crept into the woods like a voiceless assailant, slithering in where it didn't belong. She could see orbs out there. Round iridescent animal eyes glowing in the darkness.

Nicole walked to the edge of the woods and squinted into the dark. Was the house she'd seen in her dream there? A stone house hidden in the woods. She could feel it, shifting in and out of the trees. It felt closer now than it had before.

Her mind slid to Steve, who somehow felt farther than he had before. He was at home now; she could almost see him at the kitchen table staring off into space. Things had been going well for them in Lilin up until now. Nicole wondered how far out of his vision of her she could wander before he would lose her entirely, before he stopped recognizing her. They'd been together for what felt like a long time, but she could see now that it was short—painfully short. She'd run directly from a wrecked home into his home as fast as she could. And Steve had been there to tell her what was right, to scoop her up and whisk her away to a new town and tell her it was home. And she wanted to believe—who doesn't want to believe in home?

There was someone in the woods. She hadn't seen them at first, however now it was so obvious she felt like a fool. There, in among the trees, being so still.

"Hello?" she called.

The person did not move, except she plainly saw them blink.

"I can see you. It's okay. I'm here too."

They shifted in the darkness, the features coming into focus then blurring back into their camouflage like a chameleon shifting positions. It was a man. Nicole took a step forward. Her heart bucked, telling her how stupid this was, how this could be anyone—including a murderer. She moved forward anyway. The man took a step back and Nicole almost lost his face, and losing it scared her even more. If he got away from her, he could be anywhere. She moved backward, out of the woods, toward the glaring blue-white cross. She backed away until she bumped into the side of the church and screamed. The bright animal instinct inside her brain told her to flee and she obeyed. She raced to her car, gravel spraying away from her sneakers as she ran.

Once inside she locked the doors and waited, huffing,

to see if anyone was coming for her. All she heard were crickets. Her first instinct was to call the police, but that wasn't how she handled things anymore. That sort of law no longer appealed to her. If there was a man in those woods, he'd find his way out one way or the other.

She started the car and headed toward the farm, knowing she couldn't tell Steve about any of this. Knowing he couldn't hear it. She was slipping away from him a little more every day. It wasn't purposeful, she didn't mean to be, her mind was a rushing stream—everything always running away.

CHAPTER 7

THE LADIES MET in the church parking lot so they could carpool to the hospital and then get straight to the potluck. Charity had already tasked Andrew with picking up a bucket of chicken to bring, and she felt more relieved than she expected to have one less meal to prepare. Sara had made up a pasta salad in advance and Donna baked a pie. Nicole hadn't planned anything and part of her wondered if Steve would be upset, and an even bigger part of her—a new part—did not care.

"Are we sure she's still in the hospital?" Donna asked.

"I called earlier. Room 328," Sara replied.

"We can always count on Sara," Charity said.

Nicole did not say anything, though it was clearly her turn to speak. Her eyes were on the clouds, they were moving so quickly these days. She was also holding a small plant in her lap. Sara had bought it to bring. Nicole didn't know what it was, only that it had tiny blue flowers on it and they were pretty.

"Do you think we should get balloons?"

"Jesus, Charity! Does this seem like a balloon moment?" Donna snapped.

"I don't know! I've never visited anyone who's gone through . . . a trauma."

"Who did you ask for? When you called the hospital?" Nicole asked.

"What do you mean?"

"Do we know her name? How did you find room 328? Don't you have to be family to get that kind of stuff?"

"I asked about the woman who was found outside the church. They didn't even ask who I was. I'd complain about the lack of professionalism, but it was helpful so I think I'll skip the call to the manager this time."

The clouds overhead were a little too dark to be friendly, only not so dark they needed to worry about violent storms. Maybe a rain shower. But the speed. They were racing. One wrong swirl and they'd be in trouble. Nicole held her breath for fear of stirring them up any more than they already were.

"Did the hospital say if she'd had any visitors or, you know, what her name is?"

"No, she's a Jane Doe currently. I think we should avoid using names altogether. Maybe we could call her 'miss.'"

"Is she even awake?" Charity asked. "Why are we bothering to go if she's not awake?"

"She's awake," Sara said.

"Then why don't we know her name?"

"Because she hasn't decided to tell anyone," Donna said.

"Why not?"

"Because giving away your name isn't something to do so lightly," Nicole said.

"Look, I'm just going to say it," Donna broke in. "Nicole, you're getting weird."

The sentiment was followed by a tiny "amen" from Charity and it struck Sara as funny, but she bit back the giggles.

"Lilin is getting weird."

"I guess, it still seems like you started it."

The women rode the rest of the way to the hospital in silence.

Things were getting weird.

Nicole knew she didn't start it. She was simply a symptom of weird compounding upon itself. Secrets might stay buried for a long time, but not forever. And when they came to the surface the earth around them ruptured outward. Could it have been any of them? Was Nicole a catalyst or a bystander? She was coming to terms with the answer, either way.

Hospitals smelled like the fear of death—the long ugly fight against the inevitable. Charity nibbled at the edges of her fingernails. Donna watched her in disgust. Her weakest friend putting all that frailty on display in broad daylight. She held back the urge to slap the offending hand away from her mouth.

There was a police officer sitting in a chair outside room 328. He looked at the approaching women and stood up.

"We're just here for a visit," Sara told him, smiling.

"Why's that?"

"Being neighborly."

"More like nosey."

Sara's cheeks burned like the cross outside the church she loved so much. "We happened to have found this poor soul outside our church, sir. We're charged to visit the sick and care for the . . . " The last word stuck in Sara's throat. *Dying*.

"Well, I'm charged with keeping out looky-loos. Something awful happened to this lady, and she doesn't much need a lot of hens clucking around her bedside."

"Do you think she's in danger?" Nicole asked.

"I don't have to think about that. I have to keep the population of that room down to one."

Charity couldn't make eye contact with the officer. She felt embarrassed to be there. Of course they couldn't visit. And here was Sara, standing toe to toe with him as if she had every right in the world to be there. This wasn't where Charity belonged. Looking back toward the nurse's station, she realized where she needed to be.

"Ashley?" The sound of Charity's voice startled Donna. She was about to tell her to pipe down, except Charity was already gone, wandering back down the hall to talk to one of the nurses.

"Ashley Tucker, I swear, it's been too long!"

"Oh my God, Charity! How are you?" Ashley was wearing light purple scrubs, her copper hair pulled back in a tight ponytail. The third floor had been nothing but dull ever since they settled that woman into room 328 and she was excited to finally have someone to chat with.

"I'm doing good. We were just stopping by to visit, you know. Only they won't let us inside, isn't that the strangest thing you ever heard?"

"I wish it was. They won't let us so much as check her vitals without an officer in the room, which I'm pretty certain is some sort of HIPAA violation." Ashley glared at the cop who had once again taken a seat.

"Oh, are you taking care of her?"

"If you can call it that. I wish I could do more. She's such a sad mess. I don't know what she suffered through all these years, and I don't really much want to know."

"Years?" Charity asked.

"Oh God, yeah, I heard them talking about it. That's Heather Finch, do you remember? She was a year ahead of us in school. Anyway, she went missing a couple years ago and everyone thought she ran off with that kid from the grocery store." The other women had abandoned room 328 for the gossip session Charity was currently holding.

"The football player?" Charity asked.

"Absolutely! Everyone knew they were screwing around, which, gross. You know? And he went off to college—pretty sure he flunked out, by the way—and then she disappears so, you know, it all made sense."

"I'd forgotten all about that," Charity said. "Or maybe tried to block it out of my memory. Talk about tacky. She must have been thirty-five and throwing herself at that kid."

"She was thirty-four," Ashley corrected. "But I guess she didn't throw herself as hard as we thought because, well, here she is. Or what's left of her. I'm telling you, Charity, she's an absolute mess."

"We brought flowers," Donna interjected. "Can we leave them with you?" She was tired of holding them.

"Oh God, sure. I'll be going in at the top of the hour. She'll probably like them."

"Has anyone else been by to visit? Her folks?" Nicole asked.

"Poor thing, she hasn't got a soul. Charity, you remember, it was just her and her daddy in school. You see her momma died; God I can't even recall when it was. Well her daddy passed last year—colon cancer."

Sara marveled at the complete lack of discretion and made a mental note to never allow this woman anywhere near her room if she was ever in the hospital.

"Is she . . . Does she talk to you?" Charity asked.

"She sure does. Although I kind of wish she wouldn't. It's enough to give a person nightmares." Ashley shuddered.

"I can't imagine who would hurt a woman like that."

"Neither can the police. It's not my place to say, but they have no idea. And Heather isn't exactly helpful."

"She doesn't remember anything?" Nicole asked.

"No, she does. She remembers everything. Only I don't think it's very helpful. Not the right details for a cop. Do you want to know what I think the oddest part is? She knows what day of the week it is."

"I don't get it," Charity said.

"Well, think about it. You're gone out of the regular world for two years. You'd think a person would kind of give up tracking time. Or not be able to, you know? I'm telling you, she showed up here knowing exactly what day of the week it was. It's spooky."

"Maybe someone told her," Sara said.

"No, it's not like that. She tells me every time I go in there. She says, 'Tuesday now, four days until Saturday.' She's always counting down to Saturday. I'm not superstitious, but I've been dreading Saturday all week."

A cold chill struck Sara's heart and she felt the sting of

tears. "Look," she said. "If we can't visit, we better get on to the church." She took the flowers from Donna and thrust them at Ashley.

"Oh, she's right, I'm sorry, Ashley. We've got to run. Hey, let's get lunch sometime soon." Charity smiled then scooted after her friends without waiting for a response.

"Charity Cole, you're a super-human gossip and I don't think I've ever been more grateful," Donna told her once they were back in the car.

"I'm not a gossip, I was catching up."

"Sure, whatever you say. Only now we basically know everything about that woman and never had to look at her."

"It's so sad, though."

"And creepy. What's with the Saturday stuff? What's Saturday?"

Nicole thought back to her day planner and all the little stars she'd marked. "It's when the church council meets."

"No it isn't," Sara blurted out.

"Um. Yeah it is?" Donna said, looking at Sara.

"I know. I just mean, that's not important."

"Maybe she went missing on a Saturday," Charity offered.

"That's probably exactly what it is," Sara said.

"I bet you're right." Nicole was certain Heather Finch had been abducted on a Saturday night. "It's pretty strange no one looked into her disappearance back then."

"It's like Ashley said, everyone thought she'd run off with that kid. I'm sure the police looked into it. I mean, they probably searched for her."

None of them wanted to talk about what might have happened to Heather in those two years while everyone she'd ever known forgot her name. A slew of unnamable horrors could take place in one hundred and four Saturdays. Forgetting made a monster bold and boldness turned men to monsters. This was the way of the world.

Steve was already at the church when his wife arrived

with the other members of the women's group. The house had become somewhat unwelcoming. His wife seemed to always be there; even when she was out, he would find her lurking in the corners.

Nicole got out of the car and hurried to her husband. She put her arms around him and pulled him in tight.

"How'd the visit go?" he asked.

"The police wouldn't let us inside the room. So, not very good."

"I didn't think about something like that."

"I guess they're worried someone might get her. Or she might get to someone."

"You can never be too careful."

"We better get inside. I don't want to miss the prayer." Nicole smiled and kissed Steve's cheek before breaking away to head into the fellowship hall.

"Steve." Sara greeted him with a small head bob.

"Hey, Sara, sorry your visit didn't go well."

"Well, it's all a matter of opinion at this point."

"Ah. A-yup. I guess that's true." Steve was getting really tired of the women in this church saying things to him that didn't make any sense. He was suddenly very excited to be at that evening's men's meeting. They didn't talk much, but at least they said what they meant.

Charity and Andrew Cole went out of their way not to sit near the Warbys at dinner. Or maybe Nicole imagined they were going out of their way. Whichever it was, they found themselves next to the Douglas family that evening. Or at least Sara and Paul. The twins seemed to have been allowed to eat with friends instead of family.

"Are you joining us tonight, Steve?" Paul asked.

"Of course. I'm looking forward to it."

"That's great. I'm glad we always have a good turnout. I was just telling Sara that the women might have better attendance if she held the meetings here instead of at home. People get nervous about going into someone's house."

"Oh, I don't know about that," Nicole said. "I bet you never met a house you couldn't enter, Paul."

Paul looked at her for a very long time.

"Honey, did you check the boys' homework before you left?" Sara asked.

"They didn't have any."

"They never do."

For a moment, Steve thought he heard wind chimes in the air.

☽☾

"Good evening, gents." Paul addressed the group. "Glad you could join me tonight. It's mighty lonely doing this all on my own." A soft chuckle. They had been here before.

"Tonight, we have some old business, some new business, and some regular old scripture business. Before we begin, does anyone have any news they need to report?"

"I think we need to address the elephant in the room." This was Charlie Whitmer.

Paul did an exaggerated look around. "The what, Charlie?"

"That woman. I heard it was Heather Finch."

Paul's eyes shifted.

"Where did you hear that?" a voice from the back of the room asked, and they all turned toward it. Reverend Grey had slipped in while they were looking for elephants.

"From my wife."

"The women are certainly stirring the pot these days," the reverend said.

"No more than usual," Paul replied. His voice was stern. "You know how they are. Talkative."

"How they are, yes. How they should be? I'm not so sure." The reverend looked down at his hands, contemplating how a wife he never had should behave. "No, I'm not so sure about that." He didn't say more, only walked out of the room, leaving the other men to clear their throats and shuffle their feet.

"It's nothing more than usual," Paul said to himself.

Steve wanted to speak up. He wanted to assure Paul that this was, indeed, more than usual. He wanted to put his arm around him and warn him that things were not okay.

"If Heather Finch came naked out of the woods behind this church, I think we ought to discuss it," Charlie began again.

"To what end?" Paul asked.

"Should we be worried about those woods, for one thing?" Andrew said. "Should our wives be worried?"

Paul looked shocked. "Your wives? Good Lord, of course not." His eyes asked them how they could think such a thing. "Heather Finch was not . . . She is not like your wives. And I think we can all agree to that."

"What's that mean?" Steve asked. "I don't know who Heather Finch is." He was learning all these details for the first time. Something told him his wife was already in the loop.

"Heather Finch was . . . " Paul stopped, not sure what language he could use inside the church. "A bit of a Mary Magdalene. If you catch my meaning." A couple of the men laughed and Paul gave them a grateful smile. "And when she disappeared, I don't think too many people gave it a second thought. She was no one."

Steve's stomach was unsettled. He had no idea who Heather was, but he didn't care for the way the men looked at each other when they talked about her. Like they loved her and hated her all in the same breath. "So," Steve muttered. "You're saying she was too slutty to care about?"

"Watch the language, Steve."

Steve's eyes widened and he laughed—a harsh ugly bark. "*My* language? You just said no one here cared when a woman from Lilin went missing. Is that how Jesus would talk?"

"We're none of us Jesus," Paul said.

"Steve's right," Charlie said. "This is not right. This is not how we're supposed to be. Not here."

"Where should we be like this?" Andrew asked. "You want us acting different in and out of church? That's pretty hypocritical."

"Oh, big word, Andy, nice work." Charlie gave a slow clap and Steve had to bite his tongue not to laugh.

Justin Marin, whose wife Donna had just come back from visiting Heather in the hospital, felt the sudden urge to defend her. "The women of this church are acting much more Christian than we are right now. They're visiting the poor woman like they ought to. We're the ones in a closed room gossiping."

"Okay, okay." Paul raised his hands and gestured them to bring it down. "Now the fact of the matter is, the church council hasn't had the opportunity to go over any of this yet, and until we do, I don't think we should be discussing it."

"What are you guys going to discuss?" Charlie asked.

"What we ought to be doing about the situation, of course. As a church, I mean."

The church council was made up of Reverend Grey, Paul, Mike Rex, and Jim Taggart. Neither Mike nor Jim took part in the men's group meetings. Steve always assumed it was because their other duties in the church took up too much of their time. Jim was the treasurer and Mike, while he didn't seem to have a job directly within the church, was old. He was old enough to be Steve's grandfather and sometimes, when he let his mind wander, he liked to think of him as such. A sweet old grandfather he never really had and equally never spoke to.

Charlie shook his head. "I don't mean any disrespect to the council, Paul. But what could you four decide that has anything to do with us or how we talk about this?"

"We'll come up with a plan."

"The women's group came up with a plan all on their own," Justin said.

"And Reverend Grey seems to think that wasn't the right plan," Andrew said.

"And Reverend Grey seems to think there are witches in the woods. Come on, guys. This is getting a little wacky." Justin was going off script.

No one spoke. The air in the room thrummed. Steve looked down at the soft carpet and wished he could burrow into it and disappear. "Maybe there are witches out there." He didn't know he said it out loud until he felt everyone's eyes on him. Now he'd gone and broken his own rules of fitting in and he silently cursed himself.

"Have you seen something?" Paul asked.

"Of course not," Steve replied. "I don't go in the woods."

"None of us should be going in those woods," Paul said. "It's not our property and not our business."

"Fine," Charlie said. "Let's sit back and do nothing for a woman who has obviously suffered and showed up at our very doorstep for help. Hey, why don't we plan a pancake breakfast or something! Raise money for a new neon cross—even bigger than the one we already have—that'll show everyone how Christian we are." Charlie stood up from the table fast enough to rock his chair backward, but not hard enough to make it topple. "I'm going home."

The other men watched him leave then looked at each other to see if any of them were bold enough to follow. None of them were.

"You know what, maybe we ought to call it a night," Paul said. His voice was softer than Steve had ever heard it. He sounded weak.

The other members of the group slowly got up and retreated. Steve found Nicole in the fellowship hall helping the toddlers glue popsicle sticks into the shape of crosses.

"Hey, we finished up kinda quick. You want to go, or are you committed?"

"Yeah, I can go. They don't really need me. The glue is nontoxic." Nicole smiled.

As they walked to the car, Steve listened hard for chimes coming from the woods, all he heard were the squirrels zipping from tree to tree. He looked at his pretty wife and smiled. He loved her. They'd had a hard time lately, and maybe that was, at least partially, his fault. Things were going to be better; he knew it. Nicole was his soulmate. God had brought them to this place together and in this place they would thrive.

CHAPTER 8

IT WAS THURSDAY NIGHT. Nicole made a tater tot casserole for dinner. Steve had worked all day and his arms and legs were tired. He'd taken a shower when he got home and now he sat with his wife at the kitchen table in a clean white t-shirt and jeans. Nicole had lit a candle earlier in the day and the smell of cinnamon apple was competing with the casserole. This was a good day.

"Did you get a lot done today?" Nicole asked. She never knew exactly what to ask her husband about his work.

"Yeah, things are going great." Steve knew Nicole didn't care about what he did out there all day. She didn't want to hear about the moisture levels of the corn.

"Are we rich yet?"

"No, not quite. I can make the tractor payment at the end of the month, so that's good."

"Do you think it's time for me to look for a job?"

"Nah, no need for that yet. You take care of the home and I'll take care of the fields. It'll sort itself out."

Nicole knew that the longer he insisted on her not working, the deeper in the hole they'd get. His father had left him a little money when he died, but most of it went to his mother, and Nicole was certain it was gone. Steve handled all the bills, and she didn't really know how their finances were, however based on the grocery budget she had she understood there were a lot of cheap casseroles and fried potatoes in her future. She didn't mind being poor, there was no sin in that, but she minded not contributing when she was perfectly able.

"Maybe just something part-time."

Steve sighed. "Let's not go down this road. We're having a good night."

"I'm not complaining."

"Listen, I'll let you know if we need any extra income. Don't worry about it. I'm not going to let us lose the farm or anything out of pride."

There it was. Pride. He knew it was a mistake to name it the moment the word left his lips. Now it hung in the air like smoke, and he squinted through it and tried to pretend it didn't sting.

"Of course, I only want you to know I'm willing, that's all." Nicole took a sip of cranberry juice and looked down at her plate. A little clump of cream of mushroom coated ground beef looked back up at her. The idea of eating it made her stomach turn and she abruptly stood from the table with her plate and carried it to the sink.

"The weather's still really mild," Steve said.

"I guess that's what you get here."

"I guess."

Nicole was standing at the sink and Steve wanted to hug her. He wanted to feel her arms wrap around him and squeeze until everything else in the world bled away and all that was left was them, threaded together. "You want to maybe have a beer with me?" he asked. "Sit out on the patio for a bit?"

"Yeah." A smile spread out across her face like warm honey. "That sounds real nice."

"Remember back when I used to smoke, and we'd sit outside together forever?"

"Of course, and after two or three beers I'd bum your cigarettes." She giggled.

"We used to have so much to talk about."

"We still do. We just don't say it anymore."

Emotion hit him and he screwed up his mouth to keep it deep where it belonged. "Let's go outside."

"Want me to run to town and get you a pack of cigarettes first?"

"Nah, that shit's no good. I know if I started up I wouldn't be able to quit."

"I was kidding."

"I know you were."

They walked out through the sun porch to the patio table. Nicole twisted the cap off her beer and took a swig.

"You know, Steve, I do love you."

"I know. I love you too." He smiled and glanced back at the house. "You know what I don't love, though," he said, hooking his thumb toward the kitchen window.

"Me leaving all the lights on?"

"No, you leaving all the cabinet doors open after you cook."

She laughed. "I like the ease of access."

"You would." He didn't know what the comment meant, although he thought it was funny. "You know, I think we are going to have a good harvest this year. Prices are up. We didn't lose much in the rainy season."

"Are you going to market soon?"

"Probably, yeah." The moon was high and bright. All the stars were gleaming. You didn't see stars like this where he grew up. The air here was different too. It was sweet. In the summer it was honeysuckle, but now it was something else. "I need another drink. Are you good?"

"Oh yeah, I'm fine."

"Be right back." Steve stepped into the house and opened up the fridge and took a quick mental inventory on how much beer was left, how many Nicole might drink, and how much money he had in the bank. He didn't like where he landed.

He twisted off the cap and tossed it in the white plastic trash can they kept next to the counter and moved to close the cabinet doors. He wanted to make a show of it in case she was watching him.

Only the cabinets were all closed.

"What the fuck?"

He closed his eyes and opened them again. Closed. Every one of them.

Confused, he wandered back outside to where Nicole was waiting.

"You know, I think maybe the house is a little drafty."

"Why's that?" she asked.

"Well, funny thing, I was going to close up the cabinets, except they're already shut. Must be a draft, right? Or maybe when I opened the back door. I know the air didn't kick on."

"What are you talking about?"

"The cabinets."

"The cabinets are still open." She pointed back at the kitchen window.

Steve's mouth went dry and he gulped his drink. There they were, wide open—gaping. Then, as if on cue, he heard Nicole's wind chimes tinkling in the trees, telling him things weren't right. No matter how much he tried to force them, things were not the same. He wished then he'd taken her up on her offer to get him cigarettes.

"I swear they were closed when I was inside."

Nicole's eyes were on him, bright and wide. He was so close. The pieces in his mind were coming together. It was only a matter of time.

"I'm starting to think I'm losing it."

"No," she told him. "No, things are finally being found."

He looked back at the kitchen window and something else caught his eye. A woman. She wandered from the kitchen into the living room and Steve lost sight of her. For a second, he thought it was Nicole then felt ridiculous because Nicole was right next to him. But things had been moving around on him lately. It was getting harder and harder to trust his senses.

"I see her too," Nicole said.

"See who?"

"You don't have to pretend. She's always been here, you just have to look."

"Please stop it." His voice was so soft. He wasn't even sure he'd spoken.

"I can't. It's too late now. Everything's already started." She stood from the table and started back toward the house.

"Nicole." His voice rose. "You're my wife! And this has got to stop."

"You'd better come inside, Steve. You don't want to get caught out after dark. Especially not tonight. She is hurrying."

He didn't want to go in there. Except the thought of being out here alone was worse. He chased after his wife. All the cabinet doors were closed. There was a light coming from the living room. A glow, like they'd left the TV on. Steve could either go toward that light or stay in the kitchen forever. In the end, he chose the light, just like they all do.

)O(

On Saturdays, Sara Douglas did the grocery shopping. She'd made her list and planned her meals and things were going exactly as they were supposed to. They were out of the brand of sausage she normally bought. She considered going with something else but chose to get bacon for breakfast instead. This was fine. It was good to have a Plan B.

At the cash register she took the grocery envelope out of her purse and thumbed through the crisp bills tucked inside. All of her money was divided among different envelopes so she never overspent. She drove home in silence.

Her twins, Rob and Josh, met her outside to take the groceries in the house. She didn't have to ask; they knew to watch for her. The boys would take everything inside and put it away for her. They didn't have many chores. At sixteen, Sara thought they should really be doing more. Although it wasn't her place to say. Paul was in charge of assigning things to the boys, of doling out any needed punishments, and teaching them how to be men. Sara was in charge of cleaning their clothes, cooking their food, and checking their homework.

"How was the store?" Rob asked.

"Same as it always is."

"Can we get a snack?" Josh asked.

"There are apples and peanut butter you can have."

"Bread?"

"Yeah, that too. You know you can look. You don't need me to recite the inside of the fridge to you."

"We don't know what's safe to eat and what you're saving for dinner!" Rob protested.

Sara sighed and sat on the couch. She needed to go over the plan for Tuesday night.

"Hey, Mom, would it be okay if we went to Tommy's house tonight?" Rob asked.

"Who is Tommy?"

"Stop it, you know Tommy."

Sara grinned. She liked to tease the boys, except the older they got the less they seemed to enjoy it. "Yeah, that's fine. Are you spending the night or coming home after dinner?"

"Mrs. Oldham invited us to stay the night."

"Okay, but make sure to pack toothbrushes and good pajamas. And say thank you. And don't be pests."

"Thanks!" Josh gave her a quick hug around the shoulders before he joined his brother in their shared room.

The kids going out meant she'd be alone tonight. Saturday was church council. She could have anything she wanted for dinner, take a bath, have a nap—anything. Only something was sticking in the back of her head. She knew she couldn't stay home tonight, not with an opportunity like this gifted to her. She needed to set her mind at ease. It was silly. But sometimes people were allowed to be silly if it meant they could sleep at night.

The twins were picked up at four and she kissed Paul goodbye at five. She changed out of the navy-blue dress that buttoned down the front she'd been wearing that day and into a pair of blue jeans she usually reserved for gardening and a soft pink sweatshirt her mother had given her as a Christmas gift some years ago. Looking in the mirror, she didn't feel quite as stealthy as she hoped. Sara Douglas was not the sort of woman who owned stealthy clothes. She was the sort of woman who wore day dresses and jeans only in the garden, and when her mother had given her that sweatshirt, she'd been angry.

She drove her car to the church then realized parking in the lot with everyone else was also not stealthy, so she drove down a quarter of a mile to where three tall fat grain bins lived and pulled her car behind them. From there she backtracked to the church and was only a little out of breath by the time her sneakers crunched into the gravel parking lot.

Voices were coming from farther down the lot and she stopped so quickly she almost fell. The unmistakable silhouette of her husband stood in the calm blue illumination of the cross. She had been looking at this shadow for most of her life and knew it better than she knew her own.

"Everyone's back at the house," Paul Douglas said.

"Good," Reverend Grey replied. "I was concerned someone might not show up."

"Course not. We're all in this together. We know that."

The two men disappeared together into the woods and Sara continued standing still, afraid to make a sound. Her gut twisted with fear and regret. She shouldn't be here. She didn't want to know what was happening in these woods tonight or any other Saturday. Sleep was overrated, who needed it. Nightmares were par for the course, and she should learn to accept them. Except Sara Douglas was nothing if not stubborn, and that hard-nosed severity rose up inside her chest and told her gut to shut up. She'd made her decision and for better or worse, sicker or poorer, she would stand by it. Taking a few slow steady breaths, she told her legs to move, and they would not have thought of disappointing her.

The woods were beautiful. The soft blue light of the church crucifix decorated the trees and made the air look like magic. These were fairy woods, she told herself without knowing what it meant. She stopped and listened intently for the men's footsteps in the leaves or voices on the wind, except she couldn't hear anything. Better, she thought, because that meant they wouldn't hear her either.

There were fireflies in the air, but there couldn't be, it was too late in the year for fireflies. Phantom lightning bugs flitted through the trees and darted behind bushes, bathing the woods in light after the glow of the cross faded. It was greener here than it should have been. The whole area was alive and blooming. The air was sweet and warm and soft. Sara stopped listening, stopped trying to be cautious. Now she was only curious.

She walked farther into the peaceful inviting woods, following the glittering bugs. Until, without warning, they stopped. The lights blinked out and Sara couldn't see at all. She stopped and stood completely still, waiting for her eyes to adjust to the darkness. Without thinking, she had wandered away from safety. People died this way. It was horrible and awe inspiring to understand how fragile life truly was, that it could be snuffed out forever by the most inconsequential of mistakes. A wrong turn, one poor decision—any of this and more could be enough.

Sara was lost.

As her eyes adjusted, she scanned the terrain for anything familiar, futile since she'd never been in these woods before. She took a few small steps forward then stopped. What direction should she move in? After a few minutes of consideration, she decided it didn't matter. If she chose a way and stuck to it, she'd eventually come out somewhere. She was in Lilin, not the Amazon—she wouldn't be lost forever. Not like Heather Finch.

Her eyes slid up to the sky, hoping for a star to follow,

but came away empty. Only black up there. She took a deep breath and began walking again, keeping her feet low to the ground to avoid tripping. The forest was quiet now, holding its breath to see what she'd do next.

It wasn't long before she stubbed her toe on a fallen log hard enough to make her drop down to one knee. The metallic taste of blood flitted across her tongue, and she realized she'd bitten it. She closed her eyes tight for a second. The pain mixed with the panic in her belly and threatened to overtake her, she mashed it deeper down. Opening her eyes, she spat blood into the dirt and took a few deep breaths. Her eyes settled on something—something out of place. Were those shoes?

Sara leaned in close and squinted at the black, moss-covered shoes on the ground in front of her. A faraway scream carried to her on the breeze, and she bolted upright. Thick tendrils of kudzu had invaded this part of the woods. The trees in front of her were entirely overwhelmed. It spilled from the branches and danced in front of her face. Grabbing ahold of the vines, she realized there was something unusual about them, the end had been tied up into a loop. If she didn't know better, she'd think it was a noose. Fear etched lines through her veins as she came to terms with the idea that she did not, in fact, know better. This was not the right direction.

She turned around and found herself face to face with Nicole Warby. Their noses were only inches apart and Sara yelped in spite of herself.

"Who are you out here looking for?" Nicole asked, her tone casual like they'd happened upon each other at the post office.

"I'm not looking for anyone. I got turned around."

"Don't lie to me in my own home, Sara Douglas," Nicole warned. "It isn't polite."

"I'm not looking for anyone." Sara's voice was a stone wall.

"For something, then?"

"Do you know how to get out of here?"

"Do you know what happened here?"

"When?"

"What happened here before and before and before. In the long ago and much too recent?"

Sara was more afraid now than ever. Nicole was clearly losing her mind—had been for weeks—and now she was trapped out here with her, all alone.

"Dead women are practically swimming in these woods." Nicole reached out and placed her palms over Sara's eyes.

"Stop that!" Sara screamed. Nicole did not move, only pressed her hands more firmly against Sara's face. Bright colors erupted in her head but cleared just as quickly. In her mind Sara saw a little house, bright and alive. And then that same house dark and dead.

Nicole's voice followed her. "Once upon a time, a different coven lived here. Long before the Coven of the Lilin Assembly of Our Lord. But it takes effort to kill a witch. Far more effort than a rope and a fire. You must be vigilant, because no matter how deep you bury their bones, the earth will spit them back out. You can scatter their ashes to the wind, but they'll blow back into your face. You can chain them up and hurt them and make them bleed, but Sara, oh God, Sara. They will escape."

A fierce dizzying wave of nausea swept over Sara, and she dropped down onto the forest floor and retched so hard she thought she might turn inside out. When the dizziness subsided, she stayed there on all fours, spit and snot and blood oozing from her mouth and nose.

"I thought you were ready," Nicole said from above her.

"Leave me alone," Sara choked. And when she looked up, she found she was behind the grain bins, her car to the right of her. She stumbled to her feet and reached into her jeans pocket for her keys and almost cried in relief when she found them there.

The clock inside the car told her it was only 5:30. Had

she really been in those woods at all? It felt more likely that she had food poisoning. Sick or not, she knew for certain that Nicole Warby could not be trusted.

CHAPTER 9

PAUL DOUGLAS RETURNED home from the church council meeting around nine that evening. He came in quietly and called out to his wife.

"Hey," Sara said, smiling. "What's going on?"

"Reverend Grey is here with me, and I wanted to make sure you weren't in bed before I invited him in."

"That's very considerate of you. What does the reverend want?"

Paul's eyes danced. "He actually has something to talk to you about. I don't want to give anything away, but it's pretty exciting. He's waiting in his car. I'll go get him."

Sara walked into the kitchen and filled her tea kettle and put it on the burner.

"Good evening, Sara," Reverend Grey said as he entered.

"Would you like some tea? I just put the pot on."

"That sounds wonderful. Do you have anything restful? I can't have caffeine this late." He sat down at one of the bar stools that lined their kitchen island.

"Of course, I'm the same way. Although Paul tells me I probably shouldn't have caffeine any time of day. I can get a little tense." She meant it to be a joke, except it came out as more of a confession.

"We don't want to keep you all night," Paul interjected, urging them forward. "I told Sara you had something to discuss."

"I do, yes." He cleared his throat. "Sara, I know the

church has been through a lot lately. The women in particular seem to be having a difficult time."

"I don't know about difficult. But yes, some of the women do seem to be under more stress than usual. Some in particular."

"I've been doing my best to guide them these last few weeks. I've prayed and prayed on it. Truthfully, I haven't felt I was getting through."

"Oh, Reverend. Now do not think that. Your sermons are always so important. You know, I take notes on my bulletin every Sunday so I can look back on it throughout the week."

Reverend Grey smiled and nodded. "Yes, you've always been one of my most devoted. Yet I fear that not every member of the flock is as ardent. And as I prayed on the matter, the Lord was good enough to send me an answer. It seems there is a Christian Women's conference next week that's going to be discussing exactly these ideas—obedience, submissiveness, a kind and dutiful nature—and I think it's an opportunity for the women of our church. No, more than an opportunity. I think it's a message from the Lord that this has come to us at this time when we so clearly need it."

"A conference?" Sara asked. "Is it like a revival?"

"Think of it as your women's Bible study, only longer," Paul suggested.

"How much longer?"

"The conference begins Tuesday and ends on Thursday night. You'd be able to come home Friday morning."

The tea kettle whistled and Sara took it off the burner. "Come home?" she asked. "You mean we'd have to be away?"

"Yes, I'm sorry, I'm leaving things out. The conference is about two hours away and part of the participation is that you will be completely emerged in the experience. You stay on the property."

"In a hotel?" The tea bags were steeping and Sara

watched the darkness ebb from them out into the surrounding water. “Paul, we can’t afford for me to stay at a hotel for a week.”

“We wouldn’t have to,” Paul said. “The reverend has secured funding for the whole trip. It’s paid for entirely. Food, lodging, the whole nine yards.”

“What will you all do? What will everyone do? I mean, the boys can microwave some stuff, but the younger kids in the church . . . What’s everyone going to eat?”

Reverend Grey laughed and Sara had to bite her tongue. “Sara, please, don’t worry. The men of the congregation can manage the home for a few days.”

“We’ll be fine. It’ll be good for us even.”

“I guess I could freeze some casseroles tomorrow.”

Reverend Grey’s smile faded. “I know you are a strong Christian wife. And I know that you trust in the Lord and will do His will without question.”

“Yes, of course.”

“There are other women in our family who are not so strong. As a leader among them, we need you to guide them.”

Sara handed a mug to Reverend Grey and one to her husband before lifting a third mug to her lips and blowing across the surface.

“We need you to convince the ones that need convincing, basically,” Paul said. He placed his hand on her back and gently patted.

She wasn’t sure she wanted to do it, let alone how to convince the other women of the church to drop everything at a moment’s notice and leave their families for four days, to admit that would be to admit that she was not the most devout. That she didn’t trust fully in the Lord’s plan. For a split second she wondered if they’d come up with this plan while they were out in the woods together, however she pushed this away. She never saw them out there. She never went into the woods.

“I can certainly try. This is very short notice.”

"All the better," Reverend Grey declared. "If given too long to consider, people will come up with lots of excuses. I need you to trust me. This is the right thing for our church. I'm going to talk about it tomorrow morning. All I'm asking of you is to show confidence in me. In the Lord."

"Absolutely. I'm proud to stand behind my church."

"That's all I needed to hear. Thank you, truly." Reverend Grey stood up. "Now I'm afraid I've kept you all far too long. I should be getting to bed myself. We have a very big day tomorrow."

"You haven't finished your tea," Sara said.

"Another time. Thank you for your hospitality."

Once he was outside, Sara turned to her husband. "What all do you know about this conference?"

"Just what you've heard, it's to help the women find their places."

"And I need to find my place?"

"Don't be silly," Paul said. "You're going to be an example. If you didn't go, the other women wouldn't want to go, you know how it is. Charity Cole would never agree to go if you weren't there too. Lots of the ladies are like that. They need to be convinced it's right."

"And you're convinced?"

"I am."

"Well then, I guess that's all I need to hear. It'll be like a vacation."

Sara took a sip of her tea and frowned. This was all going to be very disruptive to her routine.

Reverend Grey stood before his congregation and smiled. Nicole found the smile vaguely alarming, the smile of a wolf standing before a little pig caught outside his home. The air inside the sanctuary was too warm. Steve slumped in the pew ever so slightly, his left side leaning into her right. Watching him there in front of them, ready to pounce, Nicole wanted to run. A tiny part of her worried what people would think, but she reminded herself she had already vomited in front of all of them, so what was she worried about at this point?

No, she thought. *Don't run. Let's see how this plays out.*

"Good morning," Reverend Grey said.

"Good morning," the congregation replied.

"Today I have much good news to share. But first we will turn, as always, to our scripture. I'm reading to you from Deuteronomy, chapter 18, verses nine through twelve. You may follow along. 'When you enter the land the Lord your God is giving you, do not learn to imitate the detestable ways of the nations there. Let no one be found among you who sacrifices their son or daughter in the fire, who practices divination or sorcery, interprets omens, engages in witchcraft, or casts spells, or who is a medium or spiritist or who consults the dead. Anyone who does these things is detestable to the Lord; because of these same detestable practices the Lord your God will drive out those nations before you.'

"My children, there are witches in the woods. And they are detestable. Yet I tell you they are also bold. So bold, in fact, that they would leave those woods and walk among us. Enter our community, our homes, our very church!"

There was a small flurry of whispers among the listeners and Nicole rolled her eyes. Steve must have noticed because he took that moment to squeeze her forearm. She looked at him and he raised his eyebrows at her in a way he probably thought was meaningful, but only really conveyed that he had the ability to do so.

"I have given you the Lord's instructions in order to keep these evils from you, and yet it has not been enough. The Lord has come to me, my children."

Nothing good ever followed a visit from the Lord.

"He has provided me with instructions on how to lead you from the path of wickedness and back into His glorious light.

"I will read to you now from John. 'Everyone who does evil hates the light, and will not come into the light for fear that their deeds will be exposed. But whoever lives by the truth comes into the light, so that it may be seen plainly that what they have done has been done in the sight of God.'

"This tells us plainly that those who do not follow the righteous plan of God do so because they do evil. They fear, more than anything, that their evil will be exposed and therefore will turn away."

It was beautiful. A foolproof plan to ensure that no matter what the plan was, it would be followed. Because to deny the plan would be to deny God, to shy away from the light in order to hide sin's ugliness.

"My faithful followers, God himself has shown me the way. And there is some small sacrifice involved, although I believe everyone will see how insignificant it is in comparison to the benefits. The true and devout women of this congregation have been gifted an opportunity. Those among you who are seekers of the light will be leaving on Tuesday morning for a conference. You will come back to us on Friday and you will be reborn in your faith!"

Another outbreak of hushed tones swept through the room. Was he truly sending the women of the church away with such short notice? Nicole knew what they were thinking. They were wondering who would make lunch and dinner for the kids. Who would wash the laundry and the countertops? Reverend Grey also knew what they were thinking.

"Now, I don't want anyone to worry. Your husbands and fathers want you to have this opportunity to learn and grow and come back to us all as better Christians. You will not be seen as selfish—this is not an act for yourselves, after all; it is for God Himself. As a church we will support this effort. Your way has been paid and we will be coming together to make sure no household does without in your absence."

He smiled at them, reassured them. Told them they were good to go and evil to stay. Of course, no one was forcing their hand, they did not have to attend, but why would you shy away from the all-illuminating light of the Lord?

The members of the church were a little slower to leave the sanctuary after the service. People lingered together talking, whispering.

Sara Douglas was the first person to find Nicole.

"Well," Sara said. "That was certainly exciting!"

"Was it exciting?" Nicole asked.

"I think so. I think it's a wonderful opportunity to reconnect with God. In fact, I absolutely can't wait."

"You know, neither can I."

The fixed smile on Sara's face faltered. "Really? You're planning to go?"

"Of course I am. Gosh, it's easier for me than anyone. No kids." She dropped a wink at Sara.

"Well, I'm really pleased to hear that."

"The going part, not the kids part, right?"

Sara didn't respond, just held her smile and walked away to recruit others.

"What time do you leave?" Steve asked his wife.

"You heard everything I did. I have no idea. I guess I should find out."

It was cloudy outside and the wind made it feel cooler than it was. Nicole hugged herself as she trotted over to meet Reverend Grey in the parking lot.

"Excuse me, Reverend? I was wondering what time we left on Tuesday? Are we taking a bus?"

"I'm happy to hear you plan to attend. I truly hope for you to have a transformative experience."

"Yes, it sounds like a lot of fun."

He didn't offer more, and Nicole had to restrain herself from shaking him. "So, what time?"

"We've chartered a bus to take you all promptly at five. Room for everyone."

"Five in the morning?"

"Oh yes, bright and early. It will be a perfect start to the day."

"Okay, I can work with that. Thank you, and thank you for a lovely sermon today. You know, it feels very special to be the focus of the Lord for so many weeks."

"God speaks to those who are in need."

"I thought God spoke to you." Nicole held his eyes.

"He speaks through me."

His eyes were unwavering, but Nicole still saw his secret, burning in the back of his mind. He was afraid.

"Do you hear that?" Nicole asked, tilting her ear up to the sky.

"What's that?"

"Oh, I thought I heard wind chimes. Must have been my imagination." She walked away from him and out to the car. Once inside the passenger seat, she closed her eyes and inhaled deeply through her nose before blasting loud hot air from her mouth. She did this several more times before her husband opened the driver's side door and got in next to her.

"I didn't realize you were leaving," he said, accusation in his voice.

"Sorry about that, I felt a little unsteady for a minute. I'm all better now. Did you want to go back?"

"No, we can go."

The car ride home was quiet. Nicole lay her forehead against the window and watched the grass speed by. She only had a day and a half left in Lilin before this church conference and she wanted to make the most of it. What that meant to her these days was up for debate.

The wood floors of the Warby house were dusty. The laundry had not been done. There was very little food in the refrigerator. The sink in the upstairs bathroom was crusted up with old toothpaste and grime. She could go on and on. None of these things concerned her, she didn't have the energy for them. Steve might mention them—a passive aggressive question about whether she would like him to handle the laundry, for example—but she had no intention of doing chores.

Nicole padded into the kitchen and opened what she liked to call the "medicine cabinet" where they kept the liquor. Looking over the few bottles nestled there, she settled on a half full bottle of bourbon and poured a double shot into a juice glass. Then, taking an apple from the bowl on the counter and a paring knife, she stepped out onto the sun porch and sat, munching freshly sliced bits of apple and sipping her drink.

"It's not even one o'clock," Steve said.

"I feel like a treat." She didn't look at him.

"Are you mad at me about something?"

"What could I possibly be mad at you about?"

"I'm not sure. Things haven't been going exactly right lately. And I know you wanted to join the council. And I know you probably don't want to go on whatever this trip is. I would like to talk about it with you." He sat down next to her and she cut him a thin slice of apple, which he ate without much thought.

"I don't want to be on the council anymore. I don't want you to worry about that. It's good that I'm not. And besides, they never would have let me join. I see that now. I wanted to do it to give me some kind of purpose in this town. But I think I have a different purpose now."

"What's that?" he asked though he didn't want to know.

"It's hard to explain." She took a sip of her drink and winced as it went down. Chased it with apple. "I don't want to go on this trip. Although I am. I have to. And I'm not mad at you about that, either. This is what needs to happen. The other women will need me with them."

"Can you explain to me why they need you?" He was grasping for anything.

"Moral support," she said, and burst into laughter.

"I don't want you to go," he said.

“Really? I would have thought you’d be eager at this point.” She smiled at him, but he was serious.

“I don’t want to be alone. I’ll miss you.”

“Or are you afraid of not being alone? Of being in this house with *her*?”

Steve didn’t respond.

“I don’t think she’s here for you, Steve. Not yet anyway.” Nicole stood up and walked into the house, leaving Steve to wonder who she was there for. If not him, who? He looked out into the yard where the grass ended and the thicker line of trees began. The shadows there were thick and lazy. Deep within them, something that sounded like wind chimes when it laughed abided. Sometimes it came out of the woods, yes, sometimes it did.

CHAPTER 10

THIRTEEN WOMEN FROM the Lilin Assembly of Our Lord huddled around an old school bus in the church parking lot on Tuesday morning. When the reverend had said he'd chartered a bus, this was not what they'd been expecting, however the trip was only two hours and money had likely been a concern. Their husbands stood together close by, though in a decidedly different cluster, as if they were afraid someone would mistake them for part of the trip and force them onto the rehabilitated bus.

"If we were going to ride in a school bus, I could have driven myself," Donna said, mostly to herself.

"I believe the reverend wants us to take this time to bond," Sara said, mostly to Donna.

The driver was sitting in the bus and the doors were open, but no one wanted to make the first move and actually climb on board. They waited, hushed and anxious, for a catalyst to arrive. That catalyst showed itself in the guise of Reverend Grey. He walked out of the church, his arms raised to the heavens, and addressed those gathered.

"My friends! You are here on what is no doubt the beginning of something amazing. I have been so excited for you these last days that I could hardly sleep. The chance to immerse yourself in God, to spend time devoted only to Him, this is not a gift to be taken lightly. While you are gone, your families are gladly taking on extra duties for you. They do this with a happy heart so that you may focus on our Lord. What a blessing! Go now, friends. We will meet again soon."

He gestured for them to load the bus and Sara Douglas took this as her cue to lead. She clutched her suitcase in one hand and waved goodbye to her husband with the other before stepping on board. Charity Cole followed close behind as did the others until they were all stuffed into the bus along with their luggage. It was going to be an uncomfortable ride.

Nicole was scrunched in next to a woman she did not know. She wanted to introduce herself, but was afraid they'd already met and she'd forgotten. Looking around the bus, she noticed at least five women whose names she couldn't recall—or more likely never knew in the first place. None of them had ever been to the women's group meetings. A part of the Old Nicole tried to feel superior, she squashed it down. There were more important things in life than Bible study.

And yet here they all were. Why? Did they believe Reverend Grey that their souls were in danger of being hexed? It was possible they saw this as a fun excursion out of town. They'd been given no details about the seminar other than the length of time.

Donna was behind Nicole, and she leaned forward and whispered into her ear, "Do you think there'll be a hotel bar?"

Nicole crossed the fingers of both her hands and smiled devilishly back at her. "I bet they'll give us curfews."

"You're kidding. We're adult women, for Pete's sake."

The woman next to Nicole spoke up. "When I was in high school, we'd go on some overnights with the marching band and the chaperones would put a strip of masking tape on our doors so they could tell if we'd gone out in the middle of the night."

"Yeah, but you were kids. And notoriously bad kids at that," Donna said.

"Oh, we weren't. We were just spirited."

Donna looked at Nicole, raised her eyebrows, and said, "'Spirited' in this instance means 'drum majors kept getting pregnant,' right, Tammy?"

"Oh, come on, that was one time." Tammy smiled good-naturedly and settled back against the seat, seeming to relax a little with the conversation.

"Hey, Donna?" Nicole asked. "Do you still think I started all this weirdness in Lilin?"

Donna thought for a moment. "No, maybe not. Justin and I have been talking a lot about it lately. If I'm being honest, I think maybe the church was weird before you got there. Maybe we didn't see it the same way back then. Honestly, we're thinking of leaving."

"Oh, you can't!" Tammy gasped and Donna shushed her.

"We don't want to spread it around or anything. It's not for sure. But, guys, there's a nice little Methodist church not five miles away, and my sources tell me they never talk about witches there."

"Just because they don't talk about them doesn't mean they aren't there," Nicole said.

"I guess. I'm pretty sure the Lilin Assembly of Our Lord created a few of their own through sheer force of will, though."

"That's exactly what they've done," Nicole said.

"I can't believe you're staying. If anyone has a reason to leave, it's you. The preacher called you hexed in front of the whole church."

"You did look pretty scary."

"Thank you, Tammy."

"I'm not trying to be mean," Donna said. "I'm just surprised."

"Steve really likes it there."

"Is that right? Because Justin said he got a little hot at the last men's meeting. I thought maybe you guys were thinking like we were. Things are turning sour there."

"He did? He didn't mention it." Nicole tried to imagine her husband speaking out during a church meeting and couldn't quite manage it. She'd underestimated him. A slow flush of pride heated her cheeks.

"How long is this going to take?" Tammy asked.

"About two hours, I think," Donna told her.

"Two hours, my word. We'll be sick of each other."

"It'll fly by."

They settled into silence then and watched the scenery float past. They were out of Lilin now, Nicole could feel it. On either side of the road, huge sleek white windmills appeared scattered in the flatlands that bordered the town. Three enormous arms stretched from their centers looking like a headless and crucified Titan. Nicole's eyes followed them around their slow orbit, thinking about how Lilin had brazenly created its very own witches in the woods.

The women arrived at the hotel and shuffled slowly out of the bus. Inside the lobby there was a sign proclaiming that the Women of Faith Workshop was to the right.

"Excuse me," Sara said to the woman at the desk. "I'm sorry to be a pest, we're here for the seminar and, honestly, we aren't sure how our rooms are set up. Our pastor did all of this for us and, well, we weren't given many details."

The woman frowned for a split second before her perma-smile found its proper place. "Well, let me see what I can find. Is it possibly under a group name? Or the pastor? What information can you give me?"

"We're with the Lilin Assembly of Our Lord. And it's Reverend Phillip Grey who would have made the reservations, most likely." She thought for a moment. "Or it could have also been Jim Taggart. He's the treasurer."

"That's nice." She spent a minute consulting her computer then looked at Sara again. "I think there's a problem. I don't seem to see anything with those names. Is there anything else? Who are you?"

"Sara Douglas?"

She shook her head. "Nope. You might want to call

your church and see what's happening. I'm not seeing any large block of rooms."

Sara turned back to the group that had followed her inside and forced a smile. "A little bit of confusion with the rooms. They're not ready yet; after all, it's so early. We can take our bags with us to the meeting and check in later in the afternoon."

She hoped that sounded convincing. The look Donna gave her made her think it wasn't. Nevertheless, they all turned in the direction of the meeting hall and lugged their baggage with them.

The conference room of the hotel had blue carpet and beige walls. There was a large white screen at the front of the room and five rows of long bare tables with brown folding chairs pushed up against them.

"This looks cozy," Donna said, before walking to the far side of the room and taking a seat.

There was no one else there and Sara decided to remain standing until whomever was in charge showed up, so she'd be able to greet them and introduce the group. She pulled out her phone and texted Paul, *Hotel has no reservations for us!!! Will you please get me details?*

"Was there a problem with our reservations?" Nicole asked.

"Of course not, just not ready yet. You know how hotels are, you don't check in until three or something."

"That makes sense. You know what I was thinking, no one really said we were staying at the same hotel as the meeting. It might be at a different one nearby."

"Go sit down somewhere."

At that moment a tall woman wearing a plain tan dress that came down to her calves came into the room. Her hair was intricately woven into several tight braids that wound around her head like a halo. Sara immediately took her to be the leader.

"Hello, it's nice to meet you. My name is Sara Douglas and we're all here from Lilin. I guess we're the first to arrive."

“You’ll be the only guests,” the woman said. “You can call me Jane. If you’d all take a seat, we’re going to begin very soon.”

Sara was pleased to be able to hand the reigns over to Jane. Being in charge could be tiring. She was curious why they were the only people attending but decided it didn’t matter. Maybe that’s what helped the church afford it—last-minute cancelations.

“Good morning, ladies,” Jane said, standing before them. “I want to welcome you to our little retreat. Over the next few days, you’re going to immerse yourselves in the proper and Godly lives you have been created for and you’ll unlearn the secular and evil ways this world has tried to convince you that independence and free-thinking is normal.”

A few women shifted in their seats and glanced around.

“I know what you’re thinking,” Jane continued. “You think this already sounds extreme. Don’t worry. Your lives are about to change forever.” She smiled but no one smiled back. This wasn’t selling the program quite the way she seemed to think it would. “Now the first thing is, I’m going to be collecting all cell phones and electronics.”

Charity shocked herself by blurting out, “No, I need it to check in with my kids.”

Jane frowned. “You don’t. Your husbands are taking care of the children this week. You see? Already you can see it! You don’t trust your husbands the way a Christian wife should. If you trust them, then you don’t need to check in.”

“Well, I just like to hear from them. I’ll miss them,” Charity said, a little softer this time.

“Of course you will, but you’ll be back in a jiffy to see them. You have to trust in God and your husbands, believe that they will take care of everything while you get better here with me.”

Sara raised her hand.

"Yes?"

"I do need to keep mine with me for a bit, you see, I'm waiting on a text from my husband about our hotel rooms."

"There are no hotel rooms."

"Yes, there are." Sara's frustration about the rooms was reaching a boiling point. "I need my husband to send me the specifics."

"I'm sorry, you misunderstand me. There are no hotel rooms at all. Part of your time here is staying on my farm. In fact, we'll be going there very soon. We're only meeting here for introductions."

"We have to get back on the bus?" Donna asked.

"Only a short while," Jane told her.

"Where does the bus driver stay?" Sara asked.

Jane smiled and Sara felt ridiculous for asking, yet she was confused, and it occurred to her that she didn't know who the driver was. Not that she knew everyone in Lilin, but she knew a lot.

"The driver actually lives on the farm with us. His job is to collect those who will be staying with us."

"That's very all-inclusive of you," Donna said.

"That's enough questions. I'm going to pass around a basket, and you'll all need to put your phones inside." Her voice hardened a smidge.

Sara glanced down at her phone and saw she'd received a message from Paul. *It's all taken care of, don't worry.*

Quickly she wrote back, *They're taking our phones, please let everyone know so they won't worry.*

Satisfied she'd at least helped the situation, she laid her phone in the picnic basket when it arrived in front of her. The basket made its way around the room and back to Jane, who promptly put a tiny padlock over the handle. It seemed excessive, however Sara assumed it was more symbolic than anything.

"Now, before we embark on our final journey of the day, I'd like to go around and you can all tell me your names and something you hope to gain from this time together."

A petite brunette in the front row stood up first and cleared her throat. "My name is Amber, and I'm hoping to become closer to God."

This would prove to be a very popular answer as they moved through the room. At least half of the women wanted to become closer to God. Others chose a variation, hoping to be closer to their husbands. Charity wanted to be a role model for her daughters. Sara wanted to lead others to God through her actions. Nicole Warby wanted to understand her place in the world.

"Those are all wonderful goals," Jane said. "Now, I can't promise to remember everyone's name, but I promise to try. And that's all I ask of you all during the next few days. I ask that you try."

She led them back out to the bus and the group dutifully boarded once again. They didn't know where they were going and not knowing frightened them. The fear held them together. There was a sense of comradery that they'd not experienced before. They were in this together now more than ever before. They'd put their trust in a woman named Jane whom they'd never met. For some it was exhilarating, for others terrifying, nonetheless they were together.

It took them roughly forty-five minutes to get to the farm, without their phones it was hard to be certain. No one wore a watch. Sara had tried to pay attention to what direction they were headed, and which turns they made—just in case; you could never be too careful—but it wasn't long before she'd completely lost track. This was, by itself, somehow freeing. She couldn't be responsible for them because she was equally lost.

They pulled up in front of a large one-story home. The siding was well-weathered and badly in need of paint. The front porch wrapped around the entire structure and a man sat in one of the two rocking chairs that were nestled near the front door. The rest of the farm was oddly bare. There were no animals or visible crops or even grass around the property. There was a large grey barn sitting in the midst of the dusty landscape, but it didn't look as if it had been utilized in a decade.

"You can all leave your luggage here on the bus," Jane told them. "You won't be needing it and it'll be safe here."

No one questioned the order, and this seemed to please Jane. The troops were falling in line already. She pointed to the man in the rocker as they approached. "This is Hal, you'll address him as Mr. Whitlock. He's the man of the house and we'll all treat him as such." Hal Whitlock waved to the women and a few of them waved back.

The inside of the house was simple, with raw grayed wooden floors and walls that were probably once white but had now aged to a pale yellow. A stack of tan dresses sat folded on the kitchen table. Jane pointed to them. "These are your clothes for the next few days. Everyone wears the same thing. This will keep you focused on the Lord instead of worrying with your looks. A good wife wants to make her husband proud with her appearance. You can go change, there's a bathroom down here and one upstairs. Your bedroom is down the hall there. Go make yourselves presentable then meet me back here in the kitchen and we'll begin."

The dresses did not have sizes and the ladies had to hold them up against their bodies to measure the fit. They didn't have any waist, only a straight line from the bust to the hip, and the fabric was thick and coarse. Nicole took one that was comically too large because it didn't seem to matter and wandered back toward the bedroom. She had to stifle a laugh when she saw the room. A large open space filled with bunk beds, similar to the army barracks she'd seen in movies. She did a quick count, realized some women weren't getting a bed, and wondered what the process of elimination would be.

She shoved her top over her head and flopped the new dress on with the quickness of a girl familiar with being teased about her body at summer camp. Her khakis were still on and she thought about leaving them because they weren't visible under the ankle-length dress she'd been given. In the end, she shimmied them off and folded them neatly along with her shirt and placed them on the closest top bunk. That might be enough to claim a bed, but she doubted it.

Back in the kitchen the group had mostly shuffled together again, and Nicole stood next to Sara. Jane was leaning against the counter, smiling, watching the new recruits. Her smile seemed too wide—there were not enough teeth in her mouth to support it.

"Thank you all for your cooperation so far," Jane said. "The hard parts are over now, I promise. Once you break away from your technology and your vanity, it's going to be so much easier for most of you to connect with God. You'll see."

Nicole took note of the "most of you" line and thought back to the beds.

"We're a little cramped in here, so for our first session we're going out to the barn where we can be more comfortable." Without another word she strode out the door and everyone else quietly scampered after.

The ramshackle barn was wide open; any doors it might have had probably rusted off their hinges and fell years ago. Metal folding chairs were arranged inside in several short rows, and they all sat down without being told. Some things were common sense, even in very uncommon situations.

Jane remained standing in front of them, that not-enough-teeth smile etched across her face like a jack-o'-lantern. "I've been talking with your Reverend Grey, ladies." She cut straight to the chase now. "It seems he's very concerned for your well-being. He's told me that there are witches in the woods."

Nicole glanced over at Donna. Donna, who now wanted to be a Methodist, where she hoped they didn't conjure their very own witches. Her eyes were fixed on her hands in her lap.

"He's told me there are witches and that they are no longer just in the woods!" Her voice rose. "They've escaped into your church and bewitched some of the women in this very room." Here she stopped, perhaps for dramatic effect, perhaps giving time for a surprise witch confession.

The air in the barn was motionless and so were its inhabitants. None of them looked at the others for fear they might already be looking at them. Yes, they were small town, church-going women. Yet they were not naive about what happened in the world when a woman was accused. A woman can safely be many things, but never accused.

"It is my mission in these next few days to see if you are able to be saved. We're going to pray together, work together, and learn together. And my very first prayer is that you're all able to leave this place pure."

"What if we aren't able to be saved?"

"What's your name?"

"Nicole Warby."

Jane narrowed her eyes and the last remnants of a smile finally leaked from her face. "Nicole Warby, you best pray you can be."

Now they did look because there was someone to look at. Instinct told them that there was blood in the water and if they wanted to eat, the pickings were suddenly as good as they'd get. Because they knew all too well what it meant for a woman to be accused and, God, they did not want it to be them. Anyone but them.

Nicole felt their eyes and welcomed it. Let it be her. If they must conjure a witch, let it be her.

CHAPTER 11

STEVE STAYED OUT in the fields later than usual on Tuesday, not even coming back for lunch. He'd packed a peanut butter sandwich and filled a water jug and now that it was six-thirty he was starving. But he still lingered out in the driveway. He did not want to go inside the house.

"You're being silly," he told himself.

Except every light in the house was on, waiting for him. He trudged up the front steps and leaned against the closed door and tried to think of any other options. There was nowhere else to go.

The inside of the house was hot and humid and smelled sweet and thick like being drenched in molasses. He knew there was someone in the kitchen even before he saw the impossibly tall, slender shadow stretching across the floor. He fought off the idea that he knew, because this had happened so many times before, over and over again. There was forever someone in that kitchen.

No, sometimes she was in the woods.

He walked in to meet her, and there stood Nicole. She was wearing a short black dress with a white Peter Pan collar, her blonde hair tied back in a neat ponytail. She pulled a roasted chicken out of the oven and the smell of herbs hit Steve's stomach hard.

"I thought you were at the women's meeting," he said.

"I decided you needed me more than they did."

"How did you get back?"

"I hope you're hungry. I made enough for an army."

"I'm starved."

There was a large glass bowl full of salad and she scooped some of it onto a plate and handed it to him. "Get started on this and I'll carve up the bird."

"You didn't have to come back here for me."

"I need to take better care of you, Steve. I'm your wife. Don't you want me to take care of you?"

Something in the back of his head screamed then, told him to watch his step, told him this was how it always began. "I want you to be happy," he said.

"Reverend Grey says taking care of you should make me happy."

"I don't want to have a fight. I'm happy to see you. I love you."

Nicole looked at him and grinned. "How's your salad?"

"It's good, thank you."

"Have you heard anything about Heather today?"

"Who's that? Heather Finch? That woman from the woods?"

"How quickly we forget," Nicole said. She hadn't had anything to eat yet. Steve wondered why she wasn't eating.

"I didn't forget, just making sure we're on the same page." He tried smiling. "No, I haven't heard anything. Not since the men's meeting the other night. Paul told us we weren't supposed to do anything."

"And what do you think about that?"

Steve sighed. He realized then how little he and Nicole talked these days. He wasn't sure how to talk to her anymore. Their dynamic had changed somehow in such a short time. They used to laugh and tell each other everything, but now he found himself preoccupied with whether she was supposed to know a thing, or if she would react the right way. "I didn't care for the way they were talking about her in general."

"What did they say about our poor Heather, Steve? What did those men have to say about her?"

"I don't know. It was more how they said it, what was

implied. Like she wasn't good enough to care about. It didn't sit right with me."

"You still forgot about her. You didn't like it, but you also didn't do anything."

"Hey," Steve started. He looked up at his wife and nearly fell out of his chair. For a moment, she looked like someone else. Someone he'd seen before.

Then it was over. She was Nicole, because of course she was. Except, were her eyes always brown? No one would ever call him an observant husband, but he could have sworn, would have bet money, that his wife had blue eyes. He rubbed the bridge of his nose and swiped his palms over his eyes before looking back at her. And yes, there they were—soft blue eyes, exactly like he remembered. His own eyes were playing tricks on him.

"You told them they should act better, then you also did absolutely nothing. You're letting things happen. The Bible you love so much says that faith without work is dead. Dead, Steve. It's dead."

And now her eyes were brown again, he was sure of it this time. In fact, she looked less and less like the wife he knew and believed he loved and more and more like another woman he'd seen. But where? Not here, she'd not been in this house before. But somewhere recently. On the tip of his tongue.

"I just wanted you to remember me."

"Heather?"

"Heather is dead, Steve—you let her die."

He stood up, then stopped, unsure of what he was planning to do. The gap between them was only maybe four feet and he looked at the new woman as her face shifted and blurred between personas. Eyes blue then brown then grey and other, less definable colors in between. She was hazy with brief, more terrifying moments of clarity. Without thinking he stepped forward and reached for her.

"Don't touch me," she roared. He should have felt hot

breath against his face, but there was none. "No one touches me anymore!"

Withdrawing his hand, he closed his eyes and bowed his head and prayed to nothing. There were no gods available to them this night.

Steve Warby sat at his kitchen table, eyes as blank as his mind, staring. He couldn't explain it, he liked to be idle sometimes—to be still and quiet. There was nothing wrong, or at least nothing Steve could pinpoint. His eyes were toward the wall, but also far, far beyond it. He saw nothing and so much more.

Heather Finch died at 3:27pm on Tuesday. She was alone in the hospital room where she'd been taken. No one had come to see her except the doctors and nurses. She was a relic of a past so distant everyone wished she'd stayed buried. When you exhumed these things, it reminded people of ugly truths they hoped would be forever forgotten. She brought secrets with her out of those woods, yet there was no one here to listen to them. She knew she would die with them inside of her and the knowing made her angry and bitter.

Dying itself was not so unpleasant. At first it was like getting into bed after a long day of hard work. Her limbs were heavy. Her chest sank deeper into the mattress. Keeping her eyes open became difficult, but when she closed them, she saw his face and that was too much.

He'd told her she was broken—a soft and beautiful sinner that only he could repair. Heather believed him. His hard face softened for her and when he came inside it was a baptism. He took her to the woods and made her his pet. Try as he might, he couldn't wash away her sin. She was terminally fragmented. A witch had nestled into her soul and no one, not him nor his council, could exorcise it. When the blood came, she prayed it held her evil, imagined the clots were more than tissue.

CONJURING THE WITCH

Heather was no witch.

Not yet.

As she lay there in the hospital, centuries worth of women came to her. They patted her head and whispered in her ear and told her she was innocent. The woman she once was slid away until only bitter, hot anger was left. The nurses said it was a fever, an infection, not realizing this was the virus ebbing away. The ropes that held her wrists had broken in the woods, and now the ones tied tight around her mind were rotting and slipping and falling away.

Her organs were too damaged to keep up with the demands of living. Bruised and starved and dehydrated and prodded into something like submission. The inside of her had been left to rot away while the outside was still forced to live.

What have I become? she thought. The thought was not her own. The other women were asking themselves, their wails a requiem.

How long does it take a person to forget themselves? How many weeks and months does it take the mind to break? When you brand them witches, how long before they become just that?

Heather Finch was no witch, no sinner, no source of evil. She had not been broken when she went into the woods. But that woman never left, she was still there, tied in a tiny stone house that shifted between time. She was never leaving. Soon the creature they'd made there, the one that escaped, the one that lay dying in a hospital room, would return to the woods. The only home it remembered.

In the woods they'd conjured the witch. And now she was among them.

CHAPTER 12

THE WOMEN OF the Lilin Assembly of Our Lord were again gathered in the barn. They'd spent Wednesday morning either cleaning the farmhouse or preparing breakfast for Mr. Whitlock. Now it was time to pray.

Jane stood before them, pacing as she spoke. "The greatest priority in your life is God. Seek ye first the kingdom of God, and His righteousness. Repeat it after me! My greatest priority is God."

"My greatest priority is God," the women responded.

"Your second priority is your husband. God created you to be his companion. Always remember, you were second. Say it back, 'I am second.'"

"I am second."

"You were created from man in order to serve man. Too many of you think you're more important than you are. I see the pride on your faces. You hold yourself equal to man, but you are nothing without him. You are as worthless as a garden with no seed. Man gives you purpose."

She looked at the faces of the crowd before her and tried to gauge if her words were landing. Most of them looked only at their hands in their laps. Those women were ready. They understood their place in the world and accepted it. Others looked back into her face, eyes wide with fear—and that, too, was good. Fear could be molded. Jane could use fear.

"Without men to give purpose to your lives, you would shrivel up and return back into the earth that formed you."

Nicole raised her hand.

"You have a question?"

"Don't men also need us?"

Jane laughed, a quick, ugly bark. "Men need you to do God's will. Men need you to birth and raise their children, to prepare the meals, to clean the home. Men do not need you to give them purpose. God gives them that. You are your husband's assistant, because you do not have the God-given authority to lead."

"What about Deborah?" Nicole asked.

"Which one of you is Deborah?" Jane asked.

Deborah Thomas started to raise her hand, but Nicole shook her head. "Not one of us. Deborah from the Old Testament. God made her a prophet and a judge."

"Has God asked you to be a judge?"

"No."

"Then shut up. You'd be better off listening instead of questioning."

Sara was sitting to Nicole's right and she took the opportunity to step on Nicole's bare foot. It didn't hurt, but the message was clear—keep your mouth closed and your head down.

"The world has made you bold. I will remind you of the meek nature God requires of you. It is clear to me you are not yet ready to receive the Word. It is time to work. You will clean this barn. You will sweep this dirt floor until it is smooth. You will pull weeds in the yard. You will wash clothes and prepare lunch and you will learn, through servitude, where your place in this world is."

They stood to begin their chores. Sara leaned into Nicole and whispered, "Why are you doing this?"

"What am I doing?"

"You know what. You're making this harder than it needs to be."

"Sara, why are we here? This is not a Bible study!"

Sara didn't answer, because she did not know. She'd asked God that very question the night before in her prayers. Her husband had sent her here to this place with a smile on his face and she was afraid. All of her faith had been placed in her God and her husband and her reward was working barefoot in the cool air of a dirt farm.

Donna stood behind them and said, "If we make it home from this, I swear to you and God and anyone else who wants to listen, I will never set a single foot back into that church again."

"We'll be fine," Sara said, but didn't believe it. She marched to the wall and picked up one of the brooms that was propped there and began sweeping. Her practical mind told her to start at the back of the barn and work toward the front, yet another part of her knew it did not matter. This was not about doing a job well, it was about power, and the wives and mothers of Lilin had none.

Charity hurried to the kitchen to help make lunch. She already had a splinter lodged into the bottom of her big toe and she wasn't excited to step on any more rocks or break her nails pulling weeds. Sandwich making was something she had experience with, she could pretend her son was having a sleepover and needed snacks and that would make this feel okay. She could make all of this okay.

Jane moved from place to place, supervising the women, keeping them quiet and working. The air had taken on a chill overnight and the promise of cooler days and colder nights hung all around them. Last night the women had been allowed to share beds when it was obvious there were not enough; that would be the last time. For the next two nights the beds would go to those who were deserving and the others would sleep in the barn. They needed incentive to do well. Once it was clear there were rewards, she knew they would turn on each other, then it was only a matter of time until the wicked among them would be revealed.

All women were flawed. Jane knew this. She felt it in her own blood, snaking like smoke in her veins. This farm was her penance to the Lord for her own wickedness. It had been her father's, and when the well dried up and the crops turned to dust she understood it was a punishment for her sins. The animals died first, then her father, and she had been alone.

Until Hal Whitlock moved to the farm. He taught her how evil women can poison the earth and how righteous men can make it prosperous again. Her duty was to teach other evil, sinful women this lesson, and when she'd done enough, God would make things right again. She had faith.

It was simple enough to find those in need of her services. It was an act of love, sending women to her farm. For men so loved their women that they would do anything to save them—almost anything. They would send them away to be saved, but rarely did they try to do the saving themselves. It was hard work, and the wickedness inside a woman could make her cunning. It took someone who knew, who would not be swayed by large eyes and tiny smiles.

That night they all gathered in the bedroom by the light of three oil lamps and Jane told them there was not enough room at the inn. Some of them must go to the manger instead.

"We can still share," Donna said.

"You cannot. When women share a bed, sin is close at hand. Beds are for those that deserve them. Three of you will be sent out."

"Who decides?" Sara asked, already knowing.

"God decides," Jane told her. "God decides all of this. Tonight, Nicole, Sara, and Donna must go to the barn. You three have attempted to make yourselves leaders in my home—in God's home. You question and insert yourselves in matters that do not concern you. You are not opening yourself up to this experience. Your hearts are closed, and the Lord cannot get in, therefore you can also not be inside."

Sara opened her mouth to speak only to realize this was the exact wrong she was being accused of. Humiliation torched her cheeks, and she turned her eyes to the floor so she wouldn't have to meet the stares of the others. Her mind was already buzzing with ways to fix this once they were home. She needed to learn the rules of this situation and play accordingly. She could be an example of stumbling and still thriving. She was their Mary Magdalene, possessed by seven demons but made right by Christ himself. Sara of Lilin—possessed by Pride and exorcised by Jane of wherever they were.

There was one quilt for each of them out in the barn, but no pillows or any other form of comfort.

"You'll want to stay toward the back to keep the wind off of you," Jane said. "Do not be afraid or lose hope." Her voice was kind. "You can redeem yourselves. You are not being cast out into the desert for your sins. Simply spending a night in a barn with a roof over your heads. All will be well for those who have faith. I suggest you spend your prayers tonight asking Jesus to show you the true path. Good night."

The women told Jane good night and sat up, huddled together under their quilts, watching her go.

"We're all agreed this is completely insane, right?" Donna asked. "We need to get our phones back and get out of here. I didn't sign up for this and I know for certain my husband had no idea this is what we were being sent off to do."

"Do you think any of them knew?" Sara asked.

"Reverend Grey knew," Nicole said. "Maybe the entire council."

"Not Paul," Sara said, but she was unsure.

"Do we know where she put our things?" Donna asked.

"I have no idea," Nicole replied. "It's definitely back inside the house and probably in her bedroom. They aren't going to leave them sitting out on the porch for us."

This quieted them. There were no easy answers here.

"We should get some rest and try harder tomorrow," Sara said.

"Are you joking?" Donna snapped.

"I'm absolutely not. If Reverend Grey sent us here, it is part of the plan. Are all of you so far from God that you can't see his intervention?"

"Sara, this is not God," Nicole said.

"How can you be sure? How can any of us? Especially you, Nicole. If there is a witch among us, I'd lay my money on you."

"There's no such thing as witches." Donna said it loud enough to make the other two jump.

"Don't be stupid," Sara said. "There are women all over the place happily telling whoever will listen they are exactly that."

"It's not the same thing. We aren't talking about ladies out picking flowers and drinking herbal tea or whatever. They're accusing us of dancing naked with the devil and cursing folks. They're saying 'witch' when they mean 'devil.'"

"I'm not the devil," Nicole said. "I'm no witch or demon or evil spirit. But there may well be a curse on our church. One we all put there ourselves."

"I don't care. I want to go home," Donna said. "We could try walking to the closest house."

"Barefoot in the dark?"

"They can't stop us. There's just the two of them. All we have to do is say we're going, get our things, and leave."

It was so simple Donna cursed herself for not doing it immediately. Why did she ever give up her phone? She was more eager to submit than she wanted to admit. They all were. They wanted to be good and righteous—or at least appear that way.

"Tomorrow is the last full day, why don't we wait it out?" Sara suggested. "Even if you refuse to get any benefit from this, you can manage one more day."

"What if they don't send us back home Saturday morning?"

"They will. Have at least a little faith."

Sara laid her head down in the dirt and closed her eyes. She didn't want to hear any more, her mind was already too full of conflict. Questions raced through her mind. The night she thought she saw Paul going into the woods flashed across her brain. Nicole had been there, or had she? Something that looked like Nicole. No, that had been a dream, a nightmare, a moment of weakness. She'd never been in those woods. There were no ropes or shoes or councils of men inside them.

Wednesday night fellowship felt different with so much of the congregation away. There was more food from the deli than usual and two buckets of KFC. Paul added the plastic container of potato salad he'd purchased on the way over to the table and found himself a seat.

None of them had heard from the ladies that day, and while Reverend Grey told him to trust the process, he was getting a little concerned. Paul knew as well as anyone about some of the reverend's processes. He also knew this was not the time to start questioning things. In for a penny, in for a pound—and God knew he was a few pounds in at this point.

It wasn't only his wife's absence that had been keeping him awake at night. He'd received the news that Heather Finch died late Tuesday evening. That night he dreamed of being buried alive next to a rotting log deep in the woods. In his dream, Heather was sitting next to his grave, and when he awoke, just for a second, he swore he could see her in the corner of his room.

Steve Warby wasn't in attendance and that was fine with Paul. Ever since Steve's wife asked to join the council, things had been out of sorts. There had been an order to things before that. People knew their place. Now Paul was home alone and dreaming about dead women. He could stand an evening where he wasn't reminded of the unpleasant business of the council. That's exactly what it was—unpleasantness. It was something anyone outside of the council itself would never understand. There were very few people who truly understood what was meant by 'the greater good'—and even fewer who were willing to do what it took to defend it.

The reverend sat next to him and offered a small smile. Paul nodded and took a bite of the green beans on his plate.

"The congregation seems more or less content," Reverend Grey said.

"More or less," Paul agreed. Andrew Cole was the more, Justin Marin was the less. Steve Warby was an unknown factor at the moment, but he was also not there and therefore did not count.

"I love these people, Paul. I love them more than they'll ever know. We both do. All of us on the council."

Paul looked at his plate and felt sick.

"There's still work to do, you know that."

"Now isn't the time to be talking about this."

The reverend continued as if he hadn't heard. "Our flock has been happy and comfortable here for years. We knew this was inevitable, we all saw the signs. I want to know you're still willing to do the hard work. It's all fun and games in the good times, but those times ended the moment the witch came out of the woods."

"That's enough," Paul said. He locked eyes with Reverend Grey. "We all knew what we were signing up for. But part of that is a little damned discretion."

"Of course. Be ready for Saturday."

"I always am."

Paul stood before the men of the church as usual, however his heart wasn't in it. The eyes of his friends were burrowing into his skull. A light sweat broke across his brow. The idea of telling his same old jokes, leading the same meaningless discussions, felt impossible.

"Men, I know we're all a little beat right now, what with

our better halves out of town. Maybe we ought to call it a night. Say sorry to God and have a good night's sleep."

"Paul, why aren't our wives allowed to call home?" It was Justin Marin, hell bent on forcing an issue that Paul wanted to let lie.

"They're immersed in their studies. It's all part of getting closer to God. We could all do with a little less time with our phones, don't you think?"

"There's a big difference between reading gossip on Facebook and being able to call your kids, and you know that," Charlie said.

"Nobody's kids are suffering, there's no need to get dramatic. One more day and all your wives will be back home and it's going to be like they never left. You should be happy for them. Honestly, you're sounding rather selfish. It seems to me you'd want them to have this time to commune with the Lord." He thought he'd won with that. Bringing the Lord into the conversation was a surefire way to end a debate, in Paul's experience.

"Seems to me," Justin said, "that the Lord wouldn't want our wives unable to call for help right when there might be a killer roaming around."

"What killer?"

"Heather Finch wasn't mauled by bears out there in the woods, Paul. A person did that to her. And now my wife is off who knows where and I'm not allowed to call her. Doesn't seem right."

"One more day. That's all." Paul closed his Bible and walked to the door. He didn't look back and when he heard one of them call after him, he walked a little faster. The twins were sitting on the floor of the fellowship hall with three other boys, and he waved for them to follow him. It was time to go.

The reverend was right, things were not the same. He was losing his grip on the flock, and it was time to reassert it. A few weeks ago none of them would have dared question the church like this. It was time to go back in for another pound.

Steve Warby had not been upstairs since he left his bed early Tuesday morning. There was something up there. He heard it creaking around the floorboards, coming near the stairs, but not down—not yet. On Wednesday morning he'd awoken to find himself slumped at the kitchen table, his cheek mashed into the cool wood, his neck screaming. When he stretched his lower back, it burned as the blood made its way into all the nooks and crannies it had been denied. He didn't remember going to sleep at the table. All he remembered was the woman in his house.

When it was time to leave for the fields, he made himself a sandwich instead. When it was time to go to church, he made himself comfortable on the couch. Sometimes he caught the reflection in the windows of someone moving outside the house, and so he stayed inside, but not upstairs. Someone else lived there now; maybe she always had.

As night fell the wind picked up. He heard it, low and painful, whistling and whipping. He thought about Nicole and wondered if it was windy where she was, and if when she came home he would finally be allowed to leave. He haunted this house now. It had taken him days to figure it out, although now things were plain. He was the ghost slinking in the shadows, moaning in the dark. Nicole had been right all along, there were no witches in the woods.

From his spot on the couch, he could see halfway up the staircase. He listened to the pacing above him and considered if he was keeping them up there. They were trapped upstairs because he was downstairs. They were in a stalemate. The pacing stopped and Steve, too, became still, straining to hear. Slowly he rose from his seat and crept to the foot of the stairs and peered up into the dark. He crouched down to get a better view of what he thought would be the top. There were shadows on top of shadows, but no movement. And then he realized. It was too little movement, purposeful stillness. For a second, he could see the face emerging from all that dark. A glint of eyes and maybe even teeth before it retreated, and the pacing resumed. He backed away from the steps.

"There's nothing up there for you," he said.

The kitchen light was on and he knew it hadn't been before he got up from the couch. It blinked three times and went back out. His kitchen was gone now. He squinted into the room that used to house his food and saw only trees. Because he would not go to the woods, they kindly came to him. The soft blue glow of moonlit forest invaded his home. There was nothing left to do. He touched his cheeks and was surprised to feel they were wet; he didn't remember crying, but here he was. The woods enveloped him and he did not resist.

"Hello," he called to the trees.

"Hello," a voice whispered in return.

"I think I'm lost," he said.

"I think I'm lost," the voice answered.

The face now before him was not the one he'd seen at the top of the stairs, and it was not Heather Finch. It was small and soft and round. Huge brown eyes looked up into his and he guessed the girl could only be fourteen at the oldest.

"Do you live here?" he asked her.

"I do now."

"Where did you used to live?"

"No one remembers."

"Are you the witch?"

"I wish I was. She's here, though. She's not me, but she's out here. You have to listen and be so so still and then you can find her."

"I don't want to find her."

"She is hurrying."

The wind picked up and pulled at Steve's bones, making him shiver. He rubbed his arms and stupidly wished he'd thought to grab a jacket before his house turned into a forest.

The girl reached out for him and he pulled away. "You don't have to be scared of me. I can't hurt you. I wouldn't want to even if I could."

Steve took a step back all the same.

"When they brought me here it was because they were afraid. The fear made them angry. And the angry made them mean."

"Did they kill you out here?"

The girl laughed and her laughter was like wind chimes. "No, you still don't understand. They can't kill the witch. They have to hold her, keep her. Hurt her."

"I thought you weren't the witch."

"Not anymore. They lost me. It took them years, and when I died, I didn't look anything like this."

In a flash the young, sweet face changed. The bones became more pronounced, the lips thinned and cracked. Her soft, round cheeks withered, leaving sunken hollows. She lost an eye, and in its place Steve saw only a red and weeping hole. Dark earth and wriggling bugs spilled from her mouth. As fast as it happened, she was herself again, young and beautiful.

"What did they do to you?" Steve asked.

"Don't be naïve, Mr. Warby. You know the things men do to girls like me out here in these woods."

"I don't. I can't imagine . . . "

"I think you can."

Steve was silent.

"They kept her alive in me for as long as they could—feeding her all the loathing she could stand."

"Then what happened?"

"Just a little spark. A pop somewhere inside my head. It happened so fast you'd think I wouldn't have felt a thing, but I did. It was like slipping into a warm bath. And then, I was here."

"I'm sorry."

"I'm not alone, Mr. Warby. These woods are lousy with kindred spirits. And you aren't safe here." She said it so kindly.

Steve took another step back. "Why aren't I safe?"

"Because you let it happen. All of it."

"I didn't know. This isn't my fault. I don't know you!"

"What did you do?"

"Nothing!"

He screamed the word and it echoed around him like an accusation, filling the woods, flying on the wind.

"Men who do nothing are not safe in our woods, Mr. Warby. Stay away."

The forest receded slower than it had appeared. His couch took shape next to a tree, the crisp air became still as the wind rushed out of the room. All that remained was the smell of decayed bark and dead leaves. The sounds of crickets were replaced with rhythmic thumps on the floorboards overhead. Home sweet home.

He ambled to his couch and lay down. He needed to rest. Tomorrow there were things to do. Because men who did nothing were not safe.

CHAPTER 13

THE THREE EXILED women managed to sleep in short, interrupted bursts on the dirt floor of the barn. As soon as the sun rose, they shambled back toward the main house. Jane was inside sitting at the kitchen table, a steaming cup of coffee in her hands. She grinned when she saw the bleak determination on their faces, knowing it was a mask.

"I thought you'd be here earlier. Did you have a nice evening?"

"We want our phones back, please," Nicole said.

"That's not possible. I already explained to you that God wants you to connect with Him right now, not your phones. Not earthly things."

"That's fine. But we've decided we aren't doing that anymore."

"Is that so? All of you have decided this?"

"Not all of us!" Sara was quick to correct. She moved away from the other women and now stood next to Jane.

"You've turned on your friends so quickly," Jane said.

Sara faltered. She thought she was doing the right thing. "I'm turning toward God," she stammered.

Jane's grin widened and her eyes narrowed. "The deepest circle of hell is reserved for betrayers, dear."

Sara's face turned red. The blood rushed in her ears. She looked at Donna and saw only contempt in her eyes.

"Let's have our morning sermon. And after it's over, we can take a vote to see who wants their phones back and who wants to stay here and bask in the glory of the Almighty."

"I'd rather have my phone right now," Nicole said. Her jaw was set and she clenched her teeth to keep the treacherous tremble creeping into her teeth at bay.

"You can't. Listen, I run this show. And you'll have your things when I say you can. The fact of the matter is, only I know where they are and I'm not going to tell you. And not one of you is prepared to force me to tell. Isn't that right?"

Donna cut her eyes over to Nicole, looking for guidance, but Nicole was still as a statue.

"You slept in a barn last night. And maybe that made you bold enough to ask me for your things, however it certainly didn't make you any bolder than that. You didn't even come inside. And why? Because I told you not to. You've not been threatened or hurt. But you still chose to obey me, a woman you don't know. Because you have been trained to listen to the voices of this world. What I want is for you to start listening to the voice of God. Now, let's have a lesson."

Nicole still did not move. The voice inside her screamed for her to take action, to grab Jane and shake her until she relinquished their phones. But there was still another voice inside of her. A smaller, meeker voice that told her Jane was right. She was not prepared to force the issue and had no idea how far Jane would be willing to take this.

They had stayed in the barn all night.

Jane strode into the bedroom where the rest of the women were still sleeping and woke them. She passed out dry rolls to everyone to serve as breakfast, and together they trudged into the barn for their lesson.

The thirteen hugged themselves to keep warm in the cool morning light. The fabric of their dresses was thick, and for the first time they were thankful for the coarse, ugly material. Soft breaths created thick little clouds of vapor, and gathered together in the barn their heads were shrined in a soft mist.

Jane took her place standing in front of the small

congregation. Their heads were bowed, eyes lowered, hands clasped. The victory was not lost on Jane. She'd been right earlier. They thought they could come to her and demand things and she would roll over simply because she was outnumbered. None of these girls were prepared to make her do anything. And that's where they were different. Jane was prepared to do what she needed in order to save a soul. Until the others had that same confidence, Jane was in charge.

"In the beginning," she said, "God created the world. And then came man. And then finally—an afterthought of creation—came you. Woman was born of man in order to be a companion. And we fast forward a few years and here you are, turning your back on your roles. When you wake up in the morning your first thoughts are of yourselves, your needs, your small little lives. God asks so little of you, and you still deny Him."

The sky outside was a soft grey, almost the exact color of Sara's living room walls. She'd been called wrong twice in as many days and her mind was racing. She'd been wrong to lead and wrong to follow and now she looked at Nicole with red hot hate raging through her veins. This stupid girl with no family came to her church and suddenly she was lost.

"When we met, I asked you what you wanted from this experience, and you all gave me the answers you thought I wanted to hear. Or more likely the answers you wanted your friends to hear. The answers you wanted yourselves to believe. Now we are going to be more honest.

"You are here, because you were too afraid not to be. You live in constant fear, all of you. You are afraid of what people will think of you. You are afraid of gossip."

Sara turned her attention to Jane. The other women faded into the background, and it was only them now. Her hearth thumped in her chest, and she closed her eyes and listened.

"Vanity led you all here to this farm. You will leave here

humbled in the glory of God's brilliant light. Think of the time and devotion you could offer your families if you only let go of fear and doubt. This is what the Lord wants for you. He sees your true potential, but you cannot achieve it because you're all so consumed with yourselves. Wouldn't it be a relief to let go?"

A few of the women nodded.

"Yes, of course it would. And you can! All you have to do is submit to the will of your God and your master—your husband. He does not want to hurt you. He does not want to punish you, and when you obey him, he doesn't have to. You can rest easy knowing the drudgery of the day to day is lifted from you. Don't you want that?"

"I do," Charity said. Tears had made their way down her cheeks.

Donna slumped in her seat. She hated how much she liked what she was hearing. This woman was absolute evil, yet the idea of getting out of her own head was appealing. She'd been people-pleasing at this church for so long she'd forgotten what a true spiritual moment really felt like—if she'd ever known at all. When she was asked about God she could profess her faith endlessly, but how real was it? How much did she believe anymore?

"Today, you will not physically work. Today, you will simply work on your spirit. We'll do it together. There is something out there so much greater than yourself and I want to help you find it. It's my purpose on this earth to help you find it."

The women looked at her with eyes wide like saucers. They felt lost and alone in this place. They were broken, and here before them was salvation, water in the desert, a dove guiding them to the promised land. They sat empty, waiting for anyone to fill them.

"Before you leave this farm tomorrow, I will give you freedom."

"Freedom?"

All eyes turned to Nicole, who had spoken. She stood

from her chair in one smooth motion and stepped back away from the group.

"You tell them you'll give them freedom, but this is just another chain to bind them." Her voice was soft and smooth like a river stone, and deeper than usual. "Freedom does not live in servitude. Freedom is not inside a book or a church or a man. It is in your blood, where it's always been. It's screaming for you—can't you hear it?"

A low wind moaned between the planks of the barn and the twelve other women shuddered.

"You look for God inside of men, when all the secrets of the universe are inside your own cells. You've accepted their version of magic as miracle, but they are only weak tricks. You, my beautiful friends, are glorious and holy unto yourselves.

"Do not look for gods in these verses. I give you something older. I bring you a new deity, Lilin of the Forest, and her power is endless, and it is yours. You bring life to this world, yet you deny your power. You create all that you see through sheer will and still, you look to those weaker to lead you."

Jane found her voice and stamped her foot. "This is blasphemy! You will stop this right now, in the name of God I command it."

Nicole ignored her. "They know they are weak, and it makes them afraid. And from that fear they build empires and rules and a god that validates only them."

The wind outside was getting louder. Tiny stones from the barren land around the farm pelted the sides of the barn. Dust whirled in through any cranny it could find, and the room became dark.

"Don't listen to her," Jane cried. "Her evil words are bringing the anger of the Lord upon us all."

"Where are your men now?" Nicole screamed to be heard over the roar of the wind. "They've sent you away to make you docile because they fear your power. Where are they? What are those conniving little snakes up to on this night? They have gone to places they don't belong and with them they bring ruin and plague and death.

"They're in the woods. No witches, they chased them all away. They took them and held them down and stripped them and hung them naked out in their own woods. Then what's left?"

Jane ran to the barn door and yanked it open, bracing herself against the wind. But there was no storm outside the doors. She turned back to Nicole. "Witchcraft," she spat.

"I am no witch. And I am not your god." She turned back to the women of Lilin and opened her arms wide to them. "You are your own god, and that is your freedom. When you accomplish something, all glory goes to you. Don't share it with men and their weak deities. Hold your power."

"How dare you speak such evil in this house of God!" Jane screamed. "Our God has delivered us a divine prophesy that we are charged to uphold."

"What do you need in order to believe?" Nicole asked. Her skin was shimmering like hot blacktop. "Stone tablets brought down from the mountain?" The other women watched, mouths agape, as Nicole slowly lifted into the air. Soft blue flames surrounded her now, but she did not burn. "A burning bush to speak to you? No, you require a blood sacrifice. A martyr." Her body hung before them—arms outstretched, head lulling. "We have martyred ourselves thousands of times over, died for you, and you turn your eyes back to the men who nail us up."

Sara Douglas stood from her seat, openly weeping, snot and tears dripping from her chin. "I've seen them. I've seen the men going into the woods," she sobbed.

"What are they doing there?" Nicole asked.

"I don't know."

"Of course you do."

"They're taking women!"

The words rang out in the room, echoed in the rafters.

The flames around Nicole absorbed back into her flesh, her feet settled onto the earthen floor of the barn. Sara fell at her feet. Sobs racked her body.

"Stand up, Sara Douglas. Stand and speak the truth."

"I just wanted everything to be okay. I wanted . . . "

"Our comfort will not make things okay again, never again." Nicole addressed the room now. "They have martyred your sisters to appease their idea of god. They are meeting in our woods to plot their next sin. You know this is true."

"What do we do?" Donna asked, now standing next to Sara. "Call the police?"

A noise by the door drew their attention. Hal Whitlock stood there, Jane huddled behind him, a rifle in his hands. "You're going to do nothing but sit back in those chairs and shut your miserable female mouths."

"You are not welcome here," Nicole said.

"This is my barn, you stupid bitch."

"You can leave now; you still have time."

His hands were steady, and he leveled the weapon at Nicole. "Get." He motioned toward the chairs.

"Oh, Hal, you poor man. I see you." Nicole walked to him slowly. "I see the boy, unloved by the father who raised him to be hard and unfeeling. Unloved by the mother who resented him. Full of hate and fear that he will be left behind once again. That he will not be chosen."

His hands were no longer steady, and his eyes—those betrayers—shifted. "Shut up, witch!"

"Be careful, Hal, the Devil is inside her," Jane whispered.

"No devils here. We are legion." Nicole laughed and the laugh rang out, multiplied, surrounded, and morphed until it was less a laugh and more like the hollow tones of wind chimes swept up into a tornado. The end of the gun pressed into Nicole's chest. "Who are you, Hal? Who are you really? Show me."

His finger twitched on the trigger. Hal squeezed his

eyes shut against the sweat from his brow threatening to overtake them, and when he opened them again Nicole was no longer at gun's length from him, but eye to eye. There was fire reflected there and he watched in stunned, frozen horror as she leaned in, never breaking eye contact, and kissed him soft and hot on his sticky dry lips.

"Witch," he gasped.

The gun dropped from his hands and the thud as it hit the ground was dull and unimpressive. Blood flushed his cheeks and he felt, for one moment, happy. And then he felt no more. His body crumpled next to his gun, a monument to useless destruction and old, senile gods.

"Go away, Jane. Run and hide and fear for your soul."

For a moment Jane hesitated, torn between fighting the evil she saw ahead of her and mourning the man at her feet. But in the end fear won as it so often does. Because no matter how advanced we believe ourselves to be, we are simple creatures with strong survival instincts.

Turning back to the huddled women behind her, Nicole took a deep breath. "Get your things, we're going home."

CHAPTER 14

STEVE WARBY'S HOUSE was empty. He'd awoken Thursday to find his roommates had vacated. He missed them. There was no one now. His church, God, and acquaintances had left him behind. His heart mourned the loss, but he understood now. He'd been lucky enough to see into a world where others were not allowed. Shown the true light and the way. Thinking back to the start of the summer, he couldn't believe he was the same person. He was ashamed to be the same person.

There wasn't a cloud in the sky as he left home and drove his truck down to the church. The parking lot was empty, and he parked in the back and looked at the tiny church by the woods. It was smaller today. It was darker. This place he had once felt so at home in now seemed alien.

He strode to the doors, his feet crunching in the gravel as he walked. Hesitating slightly as he reached for the handle, he wondered if it would be unlocked. It was open.

"Bad men meet here," he murmured, but he glanced to the woods. Was there something out there right now? Watching him?

"Hello?" he called into the empty church.

"Hello?" the church answered him.

Reverend Grey came out of the fellowship hall and smiled when he saw Steve there. "Steve Warby! It's good that you've come. I was just praying on you."

"Is that right?"

"It is. It's exactly right. Are you here to chat? Come,

come with me into the sanctuary and we can spend some time together."

All the lights were out inside the sanctuary and Reverend Grey did not turn them on. Instead, he led the way to the altar. Steve paused on the way forward and looked at the spot where Nicole had vomited dirt all over the aisle. There was a ghost of a stain lingering there. If he focused on it long enough, he thought maybe he could still smell it.

"Pray with me, Steve."

Steve knelt down at the altar next to Reverend Grey and closed his eyes.

"Our Heavenly Father, forgive Brother Warby for his sins. Forgive him for his questioning heart and his doubts. Lift the burden of fear from his mind and show him the path of truth and righteousness. Through your everlasting grace, amen."

The room was still. Steve waited for God to reply.

"Do you speak for God, Reverend?"

"I do, in fact."

"That's good. Because I'm not hearing God so good these days. Can you interpret for me? Can you tell me the truth?"

"What truths do you seek?"

"I need to know what's in the woods."

The reverend was quiet. His looked to the large golden cross that sat at the head of the church in between the tall taper candle they lit every Sunday. "There is much to know, Steve. And knowing it is a burden I'm not sure you can carry."

"I'm already carrying a burden."

"I suppose maybe you are."

"If you tell me there's nothing out there, I'll believe you," Steve said, wishing it was true.

"Don't lie to me. Never to me, not in this place."

Steve waited in anticipation of the church coming to life around him. He held his breath and expecting some sort of anger from the God he worshipped—none came. No building had ever sounded so dead. There was no one to fear here. No deities to offend. He could tell all the lies he wanted, but all he wanted to do was cry. He sniffed back his feelings of loss and looked the preacher in the eye. "Take me to where you meet. Show me what god asks you to do there."

Reverend Grey nodded and stood. It had been so easy. Ask, and it will be given. Seek, and you shall find. Knock, and the door will be opened. Praise.

Together in silence the two men left the church and walked out into the woods. Steve had never set foot inside them before, if you didn't count the version that came to him in his home, and he didn't. The sun broke through the canopy of leaves in splotches, forcing his eyes to adjust from shade to sunlight and back again, over and over.

"Do you know what's out here?" Reverend Grey asked.

"A house?" Steve replied.

"Yes, a house. Also more than a house. There are witches in the woods. This is where we keep them, where we and others like us have kept them for generations."

"Kept people like Heather Finch?"

"Heather was only the latest, and I knew her time was coming. I could feel the power of the witch getting stronger and stronger. With each death her powers grow, and she gets closer and closer to the edge of the woods. But we can't let her escape. Do you understand?"

"Heather did escape," Steve said.

The reverend laughed. "Yes and no."

Steve was getting out of breath, but not the reverend. He'd made this walk too many times, his body conditioned. He could get there in his sleep.

A cloud passed over the sun and the landscape turned grey. Steve realized they were walking on a very narrow path. It was so subtle you'd miss it if you didn't know to look. The men who walked here did so in single file. Soft white flowers spread out from them in all directions. A lazy breeze rustled through the canopy above them, traveling forward to a place Steve had never been.

Only the door of the house was plainly visible to the casual observer. The rest of the house was shrouded in green and brown, overtaken by the forest. Nature wanted it back. But the doorway. The doorway stood clear and clean as a testament to man's power to destroy and hurt and cut back all that they see. Try as you might, precious leaves, you cannot erase what humans have carved into your flesh.

The reverend led the way into the house, Steve following at his heels. The interior was entirely dark. Reverend Grey took an electric camping lantern from a low table by the entrance and clicked it on, summoning a soft blue light in a seven-foot radius around him. The room was cool and smelled of dampness and rot and something else, something wild. Steve squinted out into the still dark areas around him and tried to adapt.

"This was the house of the witch," Reverend Grey told him.

"It's old," Steve said.

"Nearly two hundred years. And for almost as long we have held the council of Lilin here in this room."

"I don't understand," Steve said.

"Let me tell you a story, Mr. Warby. Come, sit." He motioned him forward to a table and chairs a few steps away. They were clean and decidedly less than two hundred years old. "Once a witch resided in these woods. A heathen girl who worked her magics upon the good Christian women of Lilin. She brought chaos and radical thoughts to this peaceful wood. So in order to preserve our righteous way of life, the first council met in these woods to show everyone what happened when God was mocked. Our God is one of vengeance and wrath, and he calls upon us to be his soldiers."

"They killed her?"

"Mr. Warby, a witch is not a thing to merely be killed, and besides, killing is not what is commanded of us as

Christians. No, we are commanded to be fishers of men! Our ancestors tried to save this wretched soul."

The darkness around them shimmered and Steve heard the soft echoes of screams bouncing off the stone walls. "How do you save a witch?" he asked.

"It's ugly business, Mr. Warby. Very ugly business."

"Torture?"

"That depends on your perspective."

The screams faded into pleas and then whimpers and then little more than a gentle chime on a low breeze.

"Not everyone can be saved." Steve looked back at Reverend Grey and was sickened to see he was smiling. "The body died before the soul could be rescued, and they hung what was left of her from the trees as a warning."

"She came back?" Steve asked.

"She never left. A hate that deep cannot so easily disappear. She hexed these woods and left a curse on Lilin. Her spirit is bound to this place and when she builds enough strength she can leave. So we must bind her again."

"How do you bind her?" Steve asked, already knowing.

"She attaches herself to another woman, chooses a victim to possess. It's always the same. A weak girl, one who is not strong in her faith, with questionable morals and a predisposition to dissent. And we bring that woman here to try and save her soul."

"Have you ever saved anyone?"

"The witch is strong."

"And what happens to them? The other women?"

"They stay here too."

Steve was sitting in a torture chamber. He stood from the table and tried to imagine how many horrible deeds had been committed in the space he now occupied. How many crimes had been covered and women forgotten. He wanted to run away, back to his home. and lock the doors and also forget. But forgetting was no longer an option. The banshees would come for him, screeching with claws and teeth, his wife leading the charge.

"And Nicole is next?" Steve asked.

"The witch has entered her body, it's only a matter of time. I wanted to protect her, I tried! I had hoped sending her away might be enough to change her path. Sadly, her will is strong. There is no other choice to keep the rest of us safe."

"Why would you tell me this?" Steve asked. The hairs on the back of his neck stood up.

"Nicole is different. She has too many ties here and there would be too many questions." The reverend stood next to Steve now and laid his hand on his shoulder. The lantern remained on the table and its light seemed to fade in and out. The batteries were weakening. "If you left together, it would make for a tidier package."

"We can leave," Steve said. "I can pack today. We can get out of Lilin." Steve thought about his mother, whom he had still neglected to call.

"I can't let the witch go. You know that."

The knife was buried in Steve's side before he knew what was happening. He looked down, unbelieving, as the blood soaked through his shirt and tricked down to the waist of his work pants. It should have hurt, he knew it should hurt, but all he felt was hot and then sharp as the blade sliced into his neck.

"Momma?" he whispered.

CHAPTER 15

THERE WAS NO bus to drive the women of Lilin from the farmhouse back to their church who had cast them away. Luckily, they had Sara Douglas with them. Within an hour, three large SUVs arrived, paid for by Sara's emergency credit card Paul didn't know she had. The other women did not look at Nicole as they gathered their personal items from Jane and Hal's bedroom. They were too afraid, and Nicole could not with a clear conscience tell them not to fear. Fear was their greatest ally now—it would keep them alert and awake.

Once inside the vehicle, Donna finally raised her eyes to the woman she thought she knew. "What do we do?" she asked.

"Go home. Go to your husbands and your children."

"What about the council?"

No one answered.

Charity cried softly from the back, lamenting the loss of her life before today. Only a week ago she had been happy. Only a week ago she had slept soundly at night.

"We have to do something," Donna said.

"We will," Sara said. She looked at Nicole, who only nodded.

The other women had called their families to pick them up at the church, but Nicole had not been able to reach Steve, so Donna volunteered her husband to drop her off at the farm.

"Why are you back so early? Wasn't it supposed to be tomorrow?" Justin asked.

"It wasn't as great as we were told it would be," Donna replied.

"I'm not really surprised."

"I think it's time we find a new church," Donna told him.

Nicole didn't blame Donna for still wanting a church home, a built-in community to call their own. It was a sweet idea, to find a place where they could socialize and feel safe without the constant fear of retribution. It's what they thought they'd find somewhere new, what they thought they'd had at the tiny church next to the woods. Nicole also knew the women of the church would never feel the same innocent refuge within the house of God again. One bad apple tended to spoil the bunch, and there were so many rotten apples out there. The question would always haunt them, deep in the back of their minds. *How long*? How long before the new place of worship felt too similar to the old? How long before they were commanded to submit to a master?

Steve's truck was gone, yet this alone was not unusual. He was working. He'd gone out in the fields. Nicole was keenly aware of how often he traveled out in those fields and did nothing at all, simply went to feel constructive, to stay busy. But busy was not always productive, and merely producing was not always good. Steve was out with his dirt, trying to belong in a place he did not remember.

Nicole stepped out onto the sun porch to watch night come in from the east. The wind chimes were lazy, exhausted, only lightly tinkling from time to time. She looked out to the side yard where she'd tried to plant a garden and stared. She had been there, and part of her was still there. If she tried hard enough—focused—would she be able to see herself there again? Time is not linear nor circular. It did not flow forward, yet allowed others to do so. They were trapped in moments, their brains struggling to line them up and make them orderly.

The window above her led into her bedroom, and she

had been there too, was still there, looking out at herself on the porch. She was existing on the porch and in the garden and the church and the kitchen. And in the woods. She'd never left. She could never leave.

"Anyone home?" a voice called from the side of her house, and as she gazed at the abandoned garden a man broke into her field of vision.

"I'm always home," she replied.

"I heard you'd come back early," Reverend Grey said.

"You were right."

"Can I sit with you a moment?" he asked.

"You don't have to ask. I'm your servant. But I suppose it's still polite to ask. Yes, you can sit."

"You don't believe that." He took what was usually Steve's chair across from her.

"I've heard there was a commotion at your Bible study."

"Yes, I believe the man of the house had a heart attack. It put a damper on the whole day. These things happen." Nicole met his eyes and did not look away.

"We believe that everything happens for a reason."

"That's fun."

"You don't think so?" the reverend asked.

"Children die of cancer." Nicole shrugged. "It makes the idea lose a little sparkle."

"And we believe they die for a reason. Death, even tragic death, has a purpose."

"I suppose you have to tell yourself that." The wind was still low, but the chimes were getting stronger. Reverend Grey's eyes darted to the trees. "What do you see?" Nicole asked.

"Not a thing."

"You thought you heard someone?"

"Nicole, Mrs. Warby, I'm not here on a social call. I need you to know that. I think you already do."

"You'll forgive me if I don't invite you inside."

"Your soul is in great peril." Cutting to the chase.

"Oh no."

"I have seen evil invading your spirit. We must cast it out. It is not safe."

"Of course, what should we do?"

The reverend knew it was a trick. He should have snatched her up days ago. The witch was strong inside of her now, willful. He'd allowed the council to slow him down. Paul especially had pleaded they not take a member of the church without trying first to save her. They were losing faith, all of them. They'd become weak and small and too afraid to do the work their ancestors had so selflessly shouldered.

"Don't mock me," he warned her. "I promise you will regret it."

"Are you going to drag me out of here? Do you think no one would look for me? Don't you think Steve would come for me?"

"I don't. You've been a burden to your husband for too many years. He'll be relieved to be rid of you, Mrs. Warby. And really, isn't that want you want? To take the burden from your husband? To make him happy? When he returns home today and finds you gone, he will breathe easy for the first time in years. Your last act could be one of mercy. Don't you want that?"

"No." Nicole talked slowly, making sure he heard and understood every word. "There is nothing in this world I want less. My only desire is to make the lives of the men around me less comfortable."

His hand struck out, snatched a fistful of her hair, and jerked her face toward the table. Nicole cried out less in pain or fear and more in astonishment. "Listen to me, you hate-filled bitch," he hissed. "I will drag you from this place with my own two hands. Don't think for a moment that I won't. Your time is coming." He released her hair and shook the strands that stayed in his palm to the concrete floor of the patio. "But it is not this day. No, you can sit in your home and feel haughty as a queen, but always know, I am coming."

Nicole said nothing, just watched him stand up and saunter off from where he'd come, calm and cool as a snake. She took her phone from her pocket and texted Sara.

Tonight.

She called Steve's cell phone and hung up when the voicemail picked up. Her eyes wandered up again to her bedroom window and she looked back down at herself on the patio.

"He's mad," she told herself. "But I am rage."

CHAPTER 16

NIGHT WAS COMING FAST. As Nicole got into her car to drive to the church, she considered how long it might take her to run there instead. Her body was tense and the thought of being compressed in the driver's seat made her feel antsy. But these were foolish ideas. There wasn't time to waste. Time—not a circle, not a line—was pushing her onward to the next moment. At the farmhouse, Jane had told her she was not prepared to do certain things, but she'd proved Jane wrong.

Steve's truck was waiting for her in the church parking lot and Nicole cursed him under her breath. He was waiting for her, he'd been convinced. The betrayal stung like poison and reminded her she was still very much alive, however, she wasn't entirely surprised. How could she be? She was not the wife he'd signed up for. A hot tear rolled down her cheek. She thought he was better than them, had hoped it, but in the end, he was just a man.

She got out of her car and walked to the truck, looked inside. There were no signs of life. Thursdays were quiet at the church and there were no other vehicles in sight. The great glowing cross shone out into the woods and Nicole wondered how long she could wait before the hands that had snatched her by the hair today would drag her out into them.

Sara arrived at the church minutes later, and Nicole froze when she saw someone else was in the car with her. Had everyone betrayed her?

When Donna Marin got out of the passenger side, Nicole nearly cried in relief.

"What are you doing here?"

"I've seen too much to walk away," Donna replied.

"Charity?"

"She's seen too much to not walk away," Sara answered.

Nicole nodded. She understood. These were not easy choices.

"Isn't that your husband's truck?" Donna asked.

"It is, but I don't know where he is."

The other two women were silent. They knew as well as she did what this meant. The council was by invitation only, and it seemed perhaps Steve Warby, son of Russ and father to no one, had been called to serve.

"What's the plan?" Donna asked.

"We're going into the woods," Nicole said.

"Sure, then what?"

"I want to find the house. I want to see where the church council meets."

"Do you think there will be clues out there? Something we can take to the police?"

"The police won't believe us," Sara said.

Donna didn't ask any more questions. It was clear the other women didn't have the answers. There wasn't anything they could tell her that would make this seem logical, but she was past logic at this point. Logic did not make her friend's skin burst into flame or float. From everything she'd ever learned, witchcraft was what did that. But the things she had learned also did not seem to apply. Something unexplainable was happening and she couldn't turn away from it, even if she wanted to. She would follow Nicole, at least into the woods, then make her own decision.

Sara had told her husband that she needed to go pray with Charity. He already knew about the death at the farm, but how much he truly knew she had no idea. She had never given him any reason not to trust her. She'd chosen this night as her first transgression. Like Donna, she had seen too much. The scales had fallen from her eyes.

The three women went into the woods together and they went single file.

Nicole led them and was struck by the beauty of the woods. The leaves were technicolor in the failing light, warm hues of blue and green surrounded her. The light from the church blinked out almost instantly. Lightning bugs flickered through the trees. Something else flickered through them as well, something older. It called her forward and Nicole followed.

Sara stepped in second. The woods were cool and dark. Autumn was finally catching up with them and the leaves were transitioning—not yet the bright yellows to come, but lighter than the weeks before. There was no light at all here and she kept her eyes trained on Nicole's back, the only absolute in view. She remembered the kudzu vines she'd seen the last time she was here and wondered if they'd started to brown. The forest floor crunched under foot. Somewhere ahead she thought she heard laughter, but that couldn't be right.

It was Donna's first time in the woods, and she was proud of herself for walking in without hesitation. She thought she deserved a gold star simply for this one act of bravery. At her home she'd told her husband everything that happened during the women's retreat. He listened quietly until the end. The silence after she told him about Hal's death was enormous. She knew he was asking himself the same thing she had been asking herself since it happened. Are they murderers now?

It only took a second for Sara to get lost. She looked away, half a second, at a noise to her left, then when she looked back for Nicole . . . she was gone. Behind her Donna was also gone and Sara stopped so quickly she almost fell over.

"Donna?" she called.

Nothing.

"Nicole?"

Nothing.

"Anybody?"

"I thought you'd never ask!" A tiny young woman hopped out from behind a nearby tree and skipped over to Sara.

"Wh-who are you?" Sara asked.

"Who knows," said the girl, and she giggled.

"Did you see my friends?"

"I sure did. Don't you worry. I saw exactly where those two went. They're waiting for you. They're waiting at the house. You should hurry." The girl scrunched up her nose and grinned. "Don't be scared. I can show you where it is." She turned and jetted off into the woods.

"Wait!" Sara yelled after her. Without thinking, she dashed after the girl. What else was she supposed to do? She held her hands out in front of her to ward off the low branches that threatened her face. It didn't take long before a small house emerged in front of her. The young girl was standing next to the door, smile wide as ever.

"This is it, Sara. This is where you belong."

"How did you know my name?"

"That's our business."

Sara eyed the door cautiously.

Donna had tried to keep up when Sara took off running, but she'd lost her instantly. The old dead woods closed in around her and she pulled out her cell phone, thinking she could call her husband for help. Thinking that even if he thought she was a killer, he would still try and save her. Before she could open her contacts, a cold, strong gust of wind startled her. She looked up and found a familiar face. Except it wasn't familiar enough to place. Not at first.

The woman in front of Donna was tall and thin and very pretty. There was a nagging feeling in the pit of her stomach—she'd seen her before, recently, but not like this.

It was like seeing an old photograph of a grandparent when they were young, so familiar and yet not at all. Finally, it came to her.

"Heather?"

Heather Finch's smile was not wide. It was barely a smile at all, and the longer it sat on her face the more it resembled a grimace of pain. "You remember me?"

"Yes, of course. What are you doing here? I mean, when did you get out of the hospital?"

"Oh, Donna, they never let you out of a place like that."

Donna looked down, trying to think of a response, and instead decided to change the subject. "I've lost my friends. They were just here, have you seen them?"

Heather nodded.

"Which way did they go? Or maybe . . . Do you know which way to get out of here?"

Heather shook her head. "You can't get out. I'm really sorry. Once in, always in. I know where your friends are. I can take you there if you want. But I can't take you out of here."

Donna looked down at her phone then placed it in her back pocket. "Take me to them."

Heather sighed and then walked forward into the woods, headed toward a neglected but not forgotten tiny stone house.

Nicole couldn't believe what she was seeing. The house was beaming with light from pristine windows. The stones stood out in stark contrast from the lush forest surrounding it. It could have been constructed that very day. The door was open, and in it, a woman waited. She was thin and tall, with long red hair that hung in loose waves down to her waist. She smiled at Nicole and beckoned her forward into the light.

Inside, a fireplace sat empty—still too warm for fires. Most of the home was taken up by one large room with another door leading off from the back, presumably a bedroom.

"Do I know you?" Nicole asked the woman.

"Very well," she replied.

"Are you the witch of these woods?"

"Some would call me that. But not yet. At this time, I am simply Deborah."

"Like from the Bible," Nicole said.

Deborah shook her head. She walked to a rough wooden table and sat down. Nicole followed her, unsure what else to do.

"Is this where they killed you?" Nicole asked.

"Eventually. What I created as a refuge would one day become my prison, it's true."

"What happened?"

"The same thing that always happens, Nicole. What happens to all of us who long to be free. They called me a sinner and all the pleading and reason in the world would not dissuade them. Because men do not want reason. Men want subservience. They demand it. They came to this place and demanded I bend to the old ways. So I become something even older. Older than man and his laws."

"What do we do?"

"We rage."

Sara Douglas stepped into the dark house and swatted away cobwebs. It reeked of decay and soft wood. The nameless girl was standing in the center of the large, open room hugging herself tight.

"This house is abandoned," Sara said.

"Not quite. Someone's still here. Shhh! Listen, listen fast! You can hear her."

Sara held her breath and listened and eventually she did think she heard something. A muffled thumping coming from the door at the back of the house. Wings of panic spread out in her chest and she wanted to run, but knew she'd only be lost again if she did. She clenched her teeth together hard and balled her fists, determined not to be afraid.

"You can see her now. You're invited," the girl told her.

"I don't want to see her."

She shrugged. "You already came this far. And besides, she hasn't had company in a long time."

Sara trudged forward, feet like lead. The floorboards groaned beneath her weight. The door wasn't latched; there was no latch, barely even a door, only a slab of wood covering a door-shaped hole. With enormous strength of will she lifted her hand and pressed it against the tattered boards.

The inside of the room was pitch black and windowless. She was blind, her only compass the *thump-thump-thumping* coming from the floor ahead of her. Sara squinted into the room and crouched down, searching for whatever was making the noise. There was movement there, shadow against shadow. The air rushed in and out of her lungs in fast little puffs.

"It's not so dark," the girl said. "You can see her." The words cut through the dark like a spell and an unseen light filled the space.

Sara screamed and fell back. The person before her writhed against the ties that bound her to the floorboards. She looked at Sara with one eye, the other socket empty and leaking a dark thick fluid, like muddy soil. Her mouth fell open and an agonized wail escaped from her thin, cracked lips. Her tongue had been cut out, teeth broken, but still she thrashed, fought against the thick ropes that cut deep into her wrists, ankles, and waist. With horror, Sara realized the thumping had come from the girl knocking the side of her head against the floor over and over. A nasty bloodied bruise ebbed out from the point of contact.

Sara scrambled forward and tugged at the nearest rope, the one around her right wrist. The bindings ran through holes in the floor and looped around the girl, no visible ends to untie.

"We have to get something to cut these!" she screamed.

"No, it's okay. Just keep me company."

Sara looked back at the girl she'd met in the woods, the girl with no name. She was fading in and out like a flickering candle. "What did they do to you?"

"It's almost over now. It's so nice to have a friend here, at the end. I was so afraid to be alone."

Tears spilled out from Sara's eyes and plopped onto the bound girl's arm. She took her frail hand and held it tight.

The door to the house was open when Donna arrived. There were fresh footprints in the dirt path. "Are these yours?" she asked Heather.

"Men," Heather replied.

"Are they still here?" Donna asked, her voice dropping to a whisper.

"Only one of them. And he can't hurt you."

Despite the obvious neglect of the outside of the house, the inside was clearly in use. There was a camping lantern next to the door and she turned it on, grateful for the light. For a split second, right as the dull light clicked on, she thought she saw two women sitting at the table in the center of the room. She thought one of them was Nicole. Then they were gone.

"Your eyes will play tricks on you out here. Take care," Heather said.

The table still drew her attention. There was blood on the floor. Her feet moved back instinctively. Heather was standing next to a door at the back of the house, but Donna was afraid to go to her, afraid the blood would somehow come alive and attack. She could hear a soft smacking sound coming from that room. Her eyes pleaded with Heather. *Don't make me go in there. Don't make me see this.*

Heather didn't move and offered no comfort. There would be no encouragement here. If Donna was to move, she would have to do it on her own.

Donna Marin did not consider herself a brave woman. She was stubborn, willful, but not bold. As a child she had been curious and her constant questions had tried her mother's patience, however there were lines she never dared to cross. The fresh blood on the floor before her was one of those lines. She took another step back. Once she saw inside that room, she knew she would not be able to unsee, and everything in her life up until that moment would be different. Rose-colored memories would dim and become dark. There was still time to turn back. She could put down the lantern and retreat all the way back to her home and close her eyes and pretend it was all a nightmare.

Nicole heard something. It was coming from the bedroom. At first it was a thud, but then it became softer. She looked at Deborah, who only nodded. The strength Nicole had felt running through her veins the last few days had receded. It was outside of her now, sitting in a chair across from her, waiting, watching to see what she'd do.

Donna did not retreat, nor did she walk to the door. She ran. Holding her breath and clutching the lantern, she dashed forward, not allowing her brain time to convince her otherwise. She stood next to Heather now and Heather smiled at her. She was here. It was time to go inside.

Inside the room, Sara Douglas clutched the dying girl's hand and stroked her forehead.

"It's going to be okay," she whispered. "Everything is going to be okay."

The girl's one good eye locked onto Sara's. Her fragile body trembled and then was limp.

"Thank you," whispered the girl standing over them. "Thank you."

Sara brought her lips to the top of the dead girl's hand and kissed it lightly. It was surprisingly cold. The hand she was holding had changed. The ropes were gone, no need to tie this one down. She looked at the body next to her on the floor and saw not the sad nameless girl she'd been with, but Steve Warby, cold and dead in a pool of blood.

Sara screamed.

The scream reached Nicole and Donna at the same

time and they burst into the room almost simultaneously, crashing into each other as they fell.

Nicole looked down at her husband and wondered, *Had he been afraid?*

"Nicole," Sara sputtered. "I'm sorry, I don't know what happened."

Donna wrapped her arms around her friend and hid her face in her hair, as much for comfort as to be comforted.

Nicole felt something then, a wave of heat rolling over her. The witch. No longer at the table, no longer watching. Inside of her once again.

"I'm sorry, Sara," she said. "I'm so sorry."

And Sara, understanding completely, wept next to a man she did not love for the life of a man she believed she still did.

CHAPTER 17

IT TOOK OVER an hour for the police to find the house in the woods, and longer still for them to finally remove the body. When asked how the three women had come to find him there, they recited the same lines. Steve had not come home that day. They found his truck and searched for him.

Together?

Yes, we know there is safety in numbers, especially in the woods after dark.

Why didn't you call the police?

He hadn't been gone long. We didn't want to raise a false alarm.

Did you suspect . . .

No, never. Such a shock. Who could ever? Why would anyone?

The police notified Reverend Grey, who also came to the church. He stood in the shadows and waited. No, he'd heard no commotion. No, he'd not heard from Mr. Warby. No, he was not aware of anyone else at the church that day.

The sun spread over the Lilin Assembly of Our Lord in a blaze of reds and pinks fast and furious and the news of Steve Warby's death spread with it. Within hours a plan had come together for a candlelight vigil at the church that very night, spearheaded by the church council. A tragedy had befallen a member of the flock and it was time for the shepherd to circle the lambs.

Nicole stayed at the police station until two Friday afternoon answering question after question. They knew about the death of Hal Whitlock only hours before that of Steve Warby.

"The toxicology report for Mr. Whitlock is still at the lab," a stern detective told her. "Are we going to find anything unusual when it comes back?"

"I wouldn't know. I was told he suffered a heart attack."

"What happened out on the Whitlock farm?"

"We were having a retreat for the women. Jane and Hal were our hosts."

"And when you arrived home, where was your husband?"

"I'm not sure. I thought he must have been out at the fields. Then he didn't come home for dinner, and I got worried."

They asked her the same things over and over, but in the end, they could not hold her. She drove home in silence. There were only a few hours until the vigil for her husband. Inside the house she'd shared with him, she tried to conjure tears and failed. They would come later, now the only thing inside her was rage. It thrummed in her veins like a fever. Finally she knew the purpose her husband felt when he looked out at his farm and plunged his hands into the dirt. This was her calling.

The parking lot of the church was filled like Easter morning. Paul Douglas stood near the doorway with a box of tiny white candles held in clear plastic cups to catch the scalding wax, and he handed one to each partitioner as they arrived, offering his lighter to the first few and then letting the rest get lights from those who had arrived before.

The congregation surrounded Nicole in light and hugged her and promised her casseroles. They sang "Amazing Grace" (how sweet the sound!) and wept quietly, politely, for the young lost life. Reverend Grey stood at the edge of the woods and when the singing had subsided, he stepped forward and spoke.

"There are witches in the woods," he said, and the gathered crowd gasped. "They prey on our weakness and our sinning nature. We let them into our homes with every slight against God. When we turn from His will, we leave the door open."

Sara closed her eyes and saw a different opened door. One with a tortured young girl on the other side. Paul squeezed her hand and she felt hot bile rise in her throat, but she choked it back. She looked at her husband, the father of her children, and wondered, how much of his blood flowed through their veins? Would they grow up to be like him? Did they already know of the traditions they were expected to uphold?

"Tonight," the reverend continued, "we pray for the soul of Mr. Warby, and even more so for his young widow, who is in our midst tonight. Lord God, bring her peace. Bring her your righteous light, that she may see your plan in all of this."

As the candles sputtered out, so did the crowd. They slunk back to their safe lives with their whole and complete families and thanked God it wasn't them. They had been faithful and were spared.

"You should head on back home," Paul told his wife. "Get back to the boys."

"Aren't you coming?" she asked, already knowing.

"No, not yet. The council is holding an emergency meeting. There's a lot to discuss."

"Of course," she said. Sara drove her car down to the grain bins, the ones she'd parked next to the first night she went into the woods and sat there and waited.

"Mrs. Warby," Reverend Grey said, coming to her side. "I was hoping you might join the council in our session tonight."

"I thought women weren't allowed," she said.

"You're being invited. Since the matter at hand does concern you. You're free to say no."

“Of course. I’d be honored to attend. Thank you for the opportunity.”

Darkness closed around the church as the remaining people—the four council members and Nicole—slipped inside. The usual sounds of the woods were missing, no crickets or frogs on this night. They held their breath and waited. Somewhere, carried on a soft breeze, the phantom tinkle of wind chimes echoed.

Sara and Donna snuck back into the parking lot and stood watch outside the door.

“No one gets out,” Sara told her, and Donna nodded.

Inside, the four men and the invited woman stood in the center of the fellowship hall in a small circle.

“You know why you’re here,” Reverend Grey said to Nicole.

“I do.”

“Let us pray.” He bowed his head.

“No,” Nicole said.

The men of the room looked at her, shocked.

“I thought you said she was ready,” Jim said.

“I believed she was,” the reverend replied.

“Did we bring the ropes?” Mike asked.

“Of course,” Paul answered. “But where are we going to keep her? Has anyone thought of that? We can’t exactly go back out to the house, it’s a crime scene now. Thanks so much for that, Reverend.”

A hush fell over the room.

“She will stay in the parsonage with me, for now,” Reverend Grey finally said. “She is too strong-willed. There I can take the time to break her down.”

“No,” said Jim. “It has to be in the woods. We all know that. That’s how this works. We can’t let her out of the woods.”

“You already let me out,” Nicole interrupted. They looked at her as if they’d forgotten she was in the room and listening. She stepped into the center of the circle. “Do you think I’m afraid of you?”

"Get the ropes, Paul."

"Get the ropes, Paul," Nicole mimicked.

Paul did not move.

It was happening faster than Nicole had anticipated. She felt her skin flush the way it had in the barn. She thought she had more time, but it didn't matter. The quicker the better. She was gasoline waiting for a match.

Reverend Grey put a hand on her arm—the only spark she needed. Her skin erupted into flame, and he jumped back, yelping at the white-hot burning in his palm.

"Witch!" he spat.

"No, you stupid small man. You still don't understand. I was never your witch." The flames danced up her body, only this time was different than the barn. Her skin began to char and crack, but she felt no pain—only heat. "You and your kind cursed me for generations. You are the evil in this house, and you will burn."

Fire raced up her hair and engulfed her skull. Her clothes had burned away, and the men stared in horror as the fat and tissue melted and oozed from her blackened, broken flesh.

"Burn the witch," Nicole chanted as she moved in on the shrinking and fearful leader of men. The carpet caught fire with every step and the other men rushed for the doors, only to find them locked. "Burn the witch, burn the witch, burn the witch."

"Please," he cried, but could think of no other words.

Nicole wrapped her arms tight around Reverend Grey, swallowing him in flames. His screams ignited a renewed passion in the remaining men to escape and they beat on the door and fled to the windows. It was no use.

She dropped the shriveled, useless man and spread her arms out wide. "Burn the witch!" The voice no longer came from her burnt-out throat, but from somewhere deep inside her chest. The breastbone burst outward, and from Nicole Warby's ruined body emerged a flaming explosion of heat and rage, enveloping the room and all who cowered there.

In the parking lot, Sara saw the smoke before she smelled it.

"Now?" Donna asked.

"Not yet, we have to be certain. We can't let anyone escape."

There was screaming coming from inside the building, and also from the woods. A hundred voices full of agony cried out together and the women clapped their hands over their ears. The flames broke through the roof and lapped up into the night sky, and the higher they traveled, the quieter the screams became. Until there were none at all.

Sara took out her cell phone and dialed 911.

"Yes, there's a fire at the Lilin Assembly of Our Lord, out by the woods. Please hurry."

She shoved the phone back into her pocket and looked at Donna, who was crying.

"I think," Donna said, "the candles from the vigil must have somehow started it. Don't you?"

"Makes sense."

"Do you think it'll catch the woods on fire?"

"No, I don't think it will."

The women stepped away from the church. They could hear sirens in the distance. Sara looked out into the woods. She thought, for a second, she saw someone out there. But then it was gone. Her eyes were playing tricks on her. There were no witches in the woods. None at all.

ACKNOWLEDGEMENTS

This book began with an image of a glowing cross and a church I could not find. Now, two titles and a couple years later, it's here and I hope you've enjoyed reading it as much as I enjoyed telling it. I'd like to thank the people who made this all possible. To Max and Lori—thank you once again for believing in me and working so hard to make this book happen. I'm forever grateful to have found a publisher that cares so much about their authors. For Sean, my partner in everything and love of my life. Everything I write is driven by my desire to scare you, and in that way, you make each word a little better. Thank you to my friends who support me and urge me to be proud of my work even when I resist. Thank you to Jonathan for simply being you. And thank you, reader, for visiting Lilin with me. I've loved sharing it with you.

ABOUT THE AUTHOR

Jessica Leonard is a horror author who loves ghosts and that feeling you get when you think someone is watching you. She was born in a small town that may or may not exist and still lives there to this day. She lives with her husband, son, and two dogs. She has two novels, *Antioch* and *Conjuring the Witch*.

SPOOKY TALES FROM GHOULISH BOOKS 2023

LIKE REAL | Shelly Lyons

ISBN: 978-1-943720-82-8 $16.95

This mind-bending body horror rom-com is a rollicking Cronenbergian gene splice of *Idle Hands* and *How to Lose a Guy in 10 Days*. It's freaky. It's fun. It's LIKE REAL.

XCRMNTMNTN | Andrew Hilbert

ISBN: 978-1-943720-81-1 $14.95

When a pile of shit from space lands near a renowned filmmaker's set, inspiration strikes. Take a journey up a cosmic mountain of excrement with the director and his film crew as they ascend into madness led only by their own vanity and obsession. This is a nightmare about creation. This is a dream about poop. This is a call to arms against vowels. This is *XCRMNTMNTN*.

BOUND IN FLESH | edited by Lor Gislason

ISBN: 978-1-943720-83-5 $16.95

Bound in Flesh: An Anthology of Trans Body Horror brings together 13 trans and non-binary writers, using horror to both explore the darkest depths of the genre and the boundaries of flesh. A disgusting good time for all! Featuring stories by Hailey Piper, Joe Koch, Bitter Karella, and others.

CONJURING THE WITCH | Jessica Leonard

ISBN: 978-1-943720-84-2 $16.95

Conjuring the Witch is a dark, haunted story about what those in power are willing to do to stay in power, and the sins we convince ourselves are forgivable.

WHAT HAPPENED WAS IMPOSSIBLE | E. F. Schraeder

ISBN: 978-1-943720-85-9 $14.95

Everyone knows the woman who escapes a massacre is a final girl, but who is the final boy? *What Happened Was Impossible* follows the life of Ida Wright, a man who knows how to capitalize on his childhood tragedies . . . even when he caused them.

THE ONLY SAFE PLACE LEFT IS THE DARK| Warren Wagner

ISBN: 978-1-943720-86-6 $14.95

In *The Only Safe Place Left is the Dark*, an HIV positive gay man must leave the relative safety of his cabin in the woods to brave the zombie apocalypse and find the medication he needs to stay alive.

THE SCREAMING CHILD| Scott Adlerberg

ISBN: 978-1-943720-87-3 $16.95

Scott Adlerberg's *The Screaming Child* is a mystery horror novel told by a grieving woman working on a book about an explorer who was murdered in a remote wilderness region, only to get caught up in a dangerous journey after hearing the distant screams from her own vanished child somewhere in the woods.

RAINBOW FILTH | Tim Meyer

ISBN: 978-1-943720-88-0 $14.95

Rainbow Filth is a weirdo horror novella about a small cult that believes a rare psychedelic substance can physically transport them to another universe.

LET THE WOODS KEEP OUR BODIES| E. M. Roy

ISBN: 978-1-943720-89-7 $16.95

The familiar becomes strange the longer you look at it. Leo Bates navigates a broken sense of reality, shattered memories, and a distrust of herself in order to find her girlfriend Tate and restore balance to their hometown of Eston—if such a thing ever existed to begin with.

SAINT GRIT| Kayli Scholz

ISBN: 978-1-943720-90-3 $14.95

One brooding summer, Nadine Boone pricks herself on a poisonous manchineel tree in the Florida backcountry. Upon self-orgasm, Nadine conjures a witch that she calls Saint Grit. Pitched as *Gummo* meets *The Craft*, Saint Grit grows inside of Nadine over three decades, wreaking repulsive havoc on a suspicious cast of characters in a small town known as Sugar Bends. Comes in Censored or Uncensored cover.

Ghoulish Books
PO Box 1104
Cibolo, TX 78108

☐ LIKE REAL	16.95
☐ XCRMNTMNTN	14.95
☐ BOUND IN FLESH	16.95
☐ CONJURING THE WITCH	16.95
☐ WHAT HAPPENED WAS IMPOSSIBLE	14.95
☐ THE ONLY SAFE PLACE LEFT IS THE DARK	14.95
☐ THE SCREAMING CHILD	16.95
☐ RAINBOW FILTH	14.95
☐ LET THE WOODS KEEP OUR BODIES	16.95
☐ SAINT GRIT Censored | Uncensored	14.95

Ship to:

Name ______________________________

Address ______________________________

City____________________State________Zip________

Phone Number ______________________________

Book Total: $________

Shipping Total: $________

Grand Total: $________

Not all titles available for immediate shipping. All credit card purchases must be made online at GhoulishBooks.com. Shipping is 5.80 for one book and an additional dollar for each additional book. Contact us for international shipping prices. All checks and money orders should be made payable to Perpetual Motion Machine.

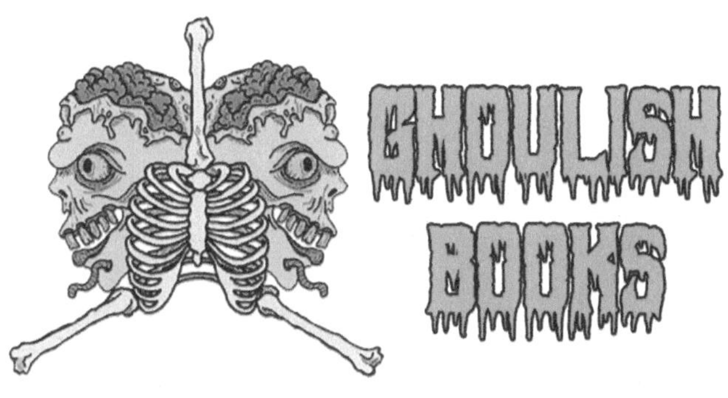

Patreon:
www.patreon.com/pmmpublishing

Website:
www.GhoulishBooks.com

Facebook:
www.facebook.com/GhoulishBooks

Twitter:
@GhoulishBooks

Instagram:
@GhoulishBookstore

Newsletter:
www.PMMPNews.com

Linktree:
linktr.ee/ghoulishbooks

www.ingramcontent.com/pod-product-compliance
Lightning Source LLC
La Vergne TN
LVHW030920080826
845145LV00013B/2987

* 9 7 8 1 9 4 3 7 2 0 8 4 2 *